MW01251921

Fuming at the Sheep

dankennedy

Knowing others is intelligence;
knowing yourself is true wisdom.
Mastering others is strength;
mastering yourself is true power.

If you realize that you have enough,
you are truly rich
If you stay in the center
and embrace death with your whole heart,
you will endure forever.

-Tao Te Ching (33)

CHAPTER ONE
MOLTING FEATHERS

On a sweltering spring afternoon, a young man in his mid twenties sits on the second to last step below the entrance of a mediocre school of law. It has been two and a half weeks since he's completed his final course. After three toilsome years he has finally received the all-important symbol of achievement and success, a diploma. They tell him he should be proud. He doesn't feel proud. He feels like the family trophy. A trophy that has been on the mantle-place for twenty-some odd years but is finally being dusted off and brought to the front. To the right sits a Boy Scouts pinewood derby first place medal and to the left a high school class ring. The young man is sitting on the proverbial docks, on the brink of stepping into a vessel that will lead him to a successful career. Another living example of the American Dream.

His classmates are ecstatic, exuberant, relieved. His teachers are relaxing for a few months or working a high profile case in order to afford the new Toyota hybrid being released next year. His grandfather has never been more proud of a grandson; his aunt has never been more proud of a nephew; his father and mother have never been more proud of anyone. Pride, Honor, Justice. He silently repeats the mantra: Pride, Honor, Justice. Pride, Honor, Justice. Pride, Honor, Justice. They fed this message since orientation and drove it home to an unconscionable extent at the commencement ceremony last night. It was as if the school's administration was under they impression that in one evening they had to refute all the negative stereotypes about attorneys to the friends and families of soon-to-be lawyers. Pride, Honor, Justice. Hearing the buzzwords so often from his professors and deans, his mind worked hard, refusing to allow them to resonate. The concepts had always made sense to him, but at this institution it was merely lip service at best, or perhaps more appropriately, at worst. Pride, Honor, Justice. Pride, Honor, Justice. He continues to repeat it, but all he can focus on is the time-honored American tradition of valuing money over happiness, and how this establishment merely perpetuates the cycle.

2

While his classmates are studying for the Bar Exam and looking for jobs with high-paying starting salaries, Kyle is sitting on the steps of a mediocre school of law touching a lit match to the corner of his diploma. As he watches the flame's evolving hue, he considers his mother and how she intends to frame this cardboard evidence of his achievement in order to place it on the wall next to hers. Another illustration of the family's emboldened success. Realizing, with a twinge of fear wrapped in a shroud of excitement, that he is now actually independent of his former life, confusion sinks in. Unshakable is the desire to appease his mother's wishes to hang his diploma like a trophy for everyone to see. Quickly, he removes a camera from his bag and snaps a photo of the smoldering flame.

As he watches the wind carry the ashes from the scorching pavement, he is reminded of the birds that dispatch their feathers every spring in the oak tree above the tire swing at his old house. He recalls how the feathers cover the grass in the backyard like snowfall. It was in this same backyard that he learned to play kickball and had his first kiss at the ripe age of fourteen. Now, with seven years of college education under his belt, he is finally granted a reprieve from stuffy classrooms. The last course he would ever take was completed several weeks ago. The graduation ceremony the prior night gave him no relief as he listened to professors, classmates, and various members of the legal community proselytize about the honor of becoming an attorney. Throughout the ceremony, Kyle couldn't disregard the knowledge that ninety-five percent of the class was just looking forward to their first big paycheck. Even those who came to law school looking for Justice and Truth, with intentions of fighting the good fight against social injustice, were boiled down, re-molded, and set aside to cool with the eventual realization that they have loans to pay so perhaps being a martyr for Justice at an income comparable to the starting salary of a McDonald's manager isn't the most practical option.

As the last bit of ash is captured by the spring's swirling winds, a student approaches Kyle and asks what he has burned. Without seeing the face of the man who's inquiry brings him back from his meditation, Kyle replies after some thought, 'Recognition of everyone's expectations of me.' Baffled, the student stares at the gentleman on the pavement for a second before walking into the school with books under his arm. Glancing up and seeing only the back of the future nobleman or magistrate, Kyle feels nothing but pity. He looks at the black mark on the pavement in front of him and smiles before making his way back to his car, with molting feathers floating behind him in the breeze.

A few days later, in a red brick house with navy shutters, a great wooden eagle sits perched above a porch bench surrounded by expensive shrubbery. Resembling a house from a catalog for a colorless monochromatic suburban utopia, the lot is missing only a white picket fence. A disgruntled mailman delivers a small package labeled 'Fragile' into the cottage-shaped mailbox adjacent to the side door.

Moments later, immediately noticing his son's handwriting staining the package, Kyle's father rushes upstairs to give the package to his wife, to whom it is addressed. With hurried precision, she opens the large envelope to find a heavy rectangle wrapped in newspaper. Taped to the front is a small envelope with 'Open This First' scrawled across the front in black marker. She rips the envelope open with excitement and frustration at so many arduous steps for communication with her one and only son. She reads it aloud without recognition of whether her husband is listening:

> *Dear Mom,*
>
> *Greetings from your long-lost son! Rather than bothering you with the prototypical allegedly polite trifles that are contained in most letters - the inquiry as to how you're doing, how the dog is doing, and how my*

father is doing - I'll get straight to the point. I know how proud you are of my recent graduation and I know you've been asking me to give you my diploma so that you can frame it and put it on the wall with yours, but that's not what I want with it. For too long now I've been allowing you to believe that this milestone is a proper occasion for pride and celebration. It isn't. This is merely a day like any other day. In fact, it's so average of an afternoon that it carries with it the standard day's tiredness and general lack of excitement. But still, I'm avoiding the point. It is important that you keep in mind that I do appreciate all that you and Dad have done for me. Please, please never lose sight of that. Now, your keen sense and motherly detective skills have probably rung an alarm in your mind, telling you that I'm about to inform you of something you're not going to be happy with. Well, sound the sirens, because here it comes. I'm not going to be a lawyer.

When you open the small package, you'll find a darling little picture frame I found at a garage sale. Within the frame you'll find what appears to be a photo of a dark crispy substance on white pavement. The ground in the picture is the pavement in front of my alma mater, and the black substance is the ashes from my diploma. While I know this is not the picture you wanted to hang above the mantle-place to show your friends and our family, (who are all sick of hearing about your lawyer-bound son, I'm sure) this photo is an accurate representation of my degree and the value that I place on it.

While you may find it difficult to believe that I have any sense of remorse or ill feelings regarding this seemingly over-dramatic action, I am, in fact, terribly sorry that this pains you. At this time it is important for you to understand what I'm doing and why I'm doing it. I figure I owe you that much, at least.

If you were to ask yourself of twenty-five years ago whether you'd prefer your future child to be happy or whether you'd rather have a lovely bronze or gold trophy to place on the mantle, which would you choose? Surely the you of twenty-some years ago would much rather have a happy child. So now I ask you: today, would you rather have a truly happy child or another trophy for above the fireplace? If your response is that you'd rather have a happy child, then this moment is surely an occasion for rejoicing. The celebration you've prepared for my recent graduation should pale in comparison to the milestone we should now be celebrating: my independence.

Now, when I say that I'm happy I'm not trying to say that I'm happy at every moment of the day, every day of the week or that I'll be happy tomorrow or ten years from now. While you may be thinking to yourself that I cannot possibly consider this blissfulness of momentary independence true Happiness, you should recognize that for the first time in a long time, we see eye-to-eye. I don't consider this happiness permanent or long lasting. However the quality of this happiness and the cause of this happiness are more important than any spell of depression I might suffer today, tomorrow, or three years from now.

Above anything and everything else, I'm taking control over my life. I'm taking back that which was never really given to me. I was once told that the Truth that you find is directly related to the amount of Knowledge you obtain. But Knowledge is not merely an accumulation of information. Knowledge is also born of experiences. Living in a beautiful home like ours - which I might add, is sorely missing a white picket fence - is not a goal in my life. I'm less concerned about my future home and more concerned about the quality of my life. But not the 'quality' you're imagining. Quality of life is not measured by material possessions or even comfort. Truth is my white picket fence. Wisdom is my dog in the yard. I'm not talking about the kind of truth that can be found in the daily newspaper or by reading volumes of literature (even if it's quality literature). What I'm getting at is a Truth that is only found through living with struggle, pain, unhappiness, happiness,

9

clarity, calmness, strife, complexities, independence, and most importantly, responsibility for the man I am and the man I choose to become. I am not merely taking control of my life; I am accepting responsibility for my life. This includes an acceptance of all the pain parents attempt to shield their children from. The yin cannot exist without the yang. The light cannot be without the dark, and I think it's about time I get out of the light and see what sort of majesty darkness holds.

It's time for me to finally take the bottle out of my mouth, spit milk in the eye of anyone who tells me not to, and get on with my life as I see fit.

I recognize that this is the most foolish decision I can make in your eyes. Now that I'm up to my neck in debt and have received a degree (in law, no less), I should suck it up and become a responsible adult and a fully functioning member of society. I should pay taxes, get married, have children, be miserable in my job, rejoice at my retirement, and lastly become bored with life and my marriage, only to live for another twenty years. You will claim irresponsibility on my part, but I can see not a single decision which is more responsible than this, and which provides more of a function to society. I'm taking responsibility for my life in the manner I see fit. I'm setting an example for all the children who have fathers that gave up their dreams in order to be practical. I'm setting an example for all the children of mothers who are no longer asked what their dreams are. I'm setting an example for the seniors who still talk about things they wish they had done, and for teenagers who are still unsure as to what they want out of life. It's not that I'm refusing to grow up, but that I refuse to give up.

The bottom line is that this is my life, and while you've supported me in every way possible throughout my life, this is a point in time where your support would be nice to have but I'm not asking for it. It's time to live for me. I'm done being a trophy to you and your parenting. If nothing else, you should be proud of this moment because your parenting (if you wish to take credit for the person I've become) has helped me get to where I am today.

I do love you, whatever that means. I appreciate you without a doubt, but I want a life of my own where I can determine the rules for myself, and that's just not part of what you were hoping I'd become.

You will not be able to get in touch with me for the next few months, and it's useless for you to attempt to contact me. I know that you're strongly opposed to my decision (especially since I haven't expressed an intent to do anything concrete), and I know that you'll still be there for me if I need you, which I appreciate but am not relying on.

Tell Dad and the dog I said Hi.

Self-Determination & Endless Possibilities,
Kyle

Since they weren't able to attend the commencement ceremony, due to Kyle's aunt being hospitalized, his parents had not communicated with their son in seventeen days (a mother always keeps track of such things). Their relief and excitement from the letter are quickly drowned by worry and doubt. Without speaking, each parent thinks back to when their son wanted to drop out of law school in his first year and how they assured him it was merely the same unsure feelings that all young professionals have. They are reminded of the few months before law school began when Kyle discussed his desire to get a philosophy degree rather than going to law school. They had brushed off these incidents as fear and typical apprehension, but considering the tone of the letter, they fully recognize that there is no talking their son out of his current mindset.

In spite of their concern for Kyle's future, and unbeknownst to each other, both mother and father experience a fraction of a second where they feel not only worry and confusion, but also a surprising sentiment of jealousy and curiosity, not withholding a twinge of resentment. They promptly suppress these unbridled emotions and find that Kyle's phone has been turned off. After leaving a message and contemplating driving the few hours to the house he has been renting with classmates, they quickly dissuade each other due to the realization that perhaps this time it is necessary to give their son space. They convince one another that he'll soon discover the harsh realities of the real world and come running back to his degree and the safety of the life they had imagined for him.

CHAPTER TWO
MEMORIES AND MISTAKES

Four months pass as if it were four days. Kyle has moved out of his shared house, much to the surprise of his ex-classmates, into a small efficiency apartment. After a few days looking for work, he finds himself moonlighting at a local grocery store for rent and food money, painting in the afternoons, taking long walks at night before work, and refusing to return calls, regardless of who the caller is. Kyle's self-contained life holds all the promises of the world. He manages to pay rent and food bills with between twenty and thirty hours of weekly work and finds himself with plenty of time to read and take the bus to the city where he can easily blend into the crowd. Downtown, Kyle can't shake the impression that everyone is rushing nowhere fast. This thought delivers to him both a sensation of importance, and a feeling of humility due to the fact that everyone around him is a self-proclaimed integral member of society. He blends into the crowd and takes his time, walking without a destination. 'At least I'm not in a hurry to get nowhere,' he thinks to himself frequently.

He doesn't mind his job at the grocery store despite the frustration born of the customers and their demands. 'Excuse me, where do you keep the toilet paper?'

'Aisle twelve.'

'Sir, do you know where I could find stencils?'

'Probably near the school supplies in the back, but you'll have to find someone in that department. They would know better than me. I don't work that side of the store.'

'Excuse me, young man, do you have any more of this coffee?'

'No ma'am, I'm sorry, we're all out.'

'What do you mean you're all out? That's the only reason I came here'

'Well, I'm sorry, but we don't have anymore. We should have more tomorrow.'

'Figures. This place never has what I come for.'

If it weren't for the customers, his job would be the easiest of unskilled manual labor work, allowing the employees to drift off into whatever world their mind cares to take them until the whistle blows. The workers quickly return home for some much needed rest after seven or eight hours of sleep-working. On one occasion, while unloading a shipment of house-wares, Kyle drifts off to a memory of the old Roman house down the street and the horror stories everyone knew so well. As the neighborhood kids had the tendency to tell it, a teenager went crazy and stabbed his family to death before turning the knife on himself. This legend explained the reason that nobody ever stayed in the house for more than a few months. Every so often the house would sell and a nice family would move in, only to quickly put the house up for sale, but not before moving out and leaving the home abandoned while waiting for a buyer. This perpetual occurrence allowed the legend to grow in the minds of the neighborhood youth. The most courageous souls on the street would run their mouths about how they would break in and show everyone that there was nothing to be afraid of, but it seemed that every time they planned the caper, a barrier was placed in their way. The self-proclaimed brave young men in the neighborhood were not able to prove their valor because of a family emergency or because they heard the house was under surveillance that night by the local police officers who had nothing better to do. Because of these all-too-frequent misfortunes, the plan was notoriously created and almost simultaneously, immediately cancelled.

One night, when Kyle was just twelve years old, he got sick of the neighborhood kids running their mouths and making excuses so he decided to check out the Roman house himself. He waited until his parents were sound asleep and snuck out of bed. Carefully creeping down the hallway, he made it downstairs without so much as a peep and glided out the front door, leaving it unlocked, as it always was.

After breaking a window and letting himself in the back door, he entered with no particular agenda and was surprised to find the lasts family's belongings still strewn about. It had been almost three months since they moved out, but all of their furniture, dishes, and most of their clothes remained in the home untouched, other than a fine layer of dust which had settled everywhere. After walking through the house with a previously unknown quantity of confidence, there was a creak in one of the walls that immediately shattered any feeling of safety Kyle managed to maintain. Deciding it was time to go, he was resolved to take something with him so the neighborhood kids would believe his heroics. Reaching on to the table, he grabbed a large pronged brass candlestick holder. As he turned to go out the back door, he heard another creak coming from the back room. Running through the living room rather than the kitchen to get to the back of the house, he tripped over the step up to the hallway and fell face first on the large brass candelabrum which he intended to take. Feeling the warmth of blood run over his upper lip, and tasting it with his tongue, Kyle wiped off his face and got up to leave. As he stood, he turned to the right and froze. Standing in front of him, eight feet away, was a boy of about fourteen years, statuesque in his lack of movement, with blood on his hands and face. Frozen for a mere moment, Kyle snapped back into the situation, hurled the candelabrum towards the figure and bolted out of the house faster than he had ever run in his life. As he took a step out of the back doorway he heard a loud crash but didn't turn around to investigate.

The following morning he told this story to the other boys in the neighborhood, who, as expected, didn't believe him due to the lack of evidence. He told them of the ghost in the house and the bloody hands. Amidst laughter, he tried to explain that he had taken something with him to prove his brave act, but had thrown it at the ghost before leaving the house. Needless to say, nobody believed him, but this further cemented their fears in the horror stories they had heard.

A few days later the local news station had a special report on a rash of break-ins in a local community. The story covered four houses that were in Kyle's neighborhood which were broken into, including the Roman house. For weeks, Kyle was terrified that the police were going to show up at his house with handcuffs, but he eluded detection. To keep tabs on the investigation, he snuck into the recycle bin and ripped out newspaper articles concerning the break-ins. He was astonished to find that none of the stories mentioned the Roman house's history of crime or the ghost stories. Leave it to the newspapers to include nothing actually newsworthy. A week and a half after the incident at the Roman house, Kyle came across an article about the supposedly haunted home. The article's author stated that she didn't think it was related to the other break-ins because the police reports stated that nothing was taken and the only thing noteworthy was the broken back door and a candelabrum lying in a pile of what was once a floor-to-ceiling mirror. Reading the article, Kyle at once realized that the ghost he had been terrified of was his own reflection. He couldn't help but laugh at his foolishness.

'Hey, be careful with those!' Knocking him out of his daydream, as usual, was his boss Phil. Phil hates his job, and attempts to remedy this by making sure that everyone around him hates their job as well. Snapped back into his work, Kyle reaches for the next box of lights coming off the conveyer belt, loses his grip, and drops it, shattering everything it contains. Surprisingly, Phil walks up to Kyle with a broom and dustpan and tells him to start cleaning the mess without so much as a furrowed brow. Finding someone else to unload the truck, Phil leaves the receiving area to have a smoke. Kyle hurries to clean the mess before his boss gets back. Just as he dumps the last dustpan of shattered glass into the trash, Phil saunters back into the loading dock, takes the broom from Kyle's hand and tells him to go home and that his last paycheck would be in the mail.

Never one for confrontation, and shocked by Phil's good temperament in doing such a horrid thing, Kyle meekly exits the back room without uttering a word or casting so much as a sideways glance in Phil's direction. Knowing he needs the job, but feeling terrifyingly liberated, Kyle fights off the urge to plead for his employment. As he walks through the store, a typical, but not often found in Kyle, alpha male pride kicks in and he unearths the resolve to brood rather than beg, and further vows never to set foot in the store again.

CHAPTER THREE
THE PASSIONATE PREACHER

Walking out of his building's front door, the sun and wind hit Kyle in the face just as fiercely as his newly acquired freedom did exactly a week prior when he got fired from the grocery store. The leaves swirl around his shoes while he crosses the street and enters the large park he frequents. He immediately notices two gentlemen by the fountain engaged a conversation that, based on the body language and the few bits of conversation he manages to hear, is both passionate and reverent. Always a fan of eavesdropping, the young man nonchalantly meanders within earshot and takes a seat on a nearby bench.

'I know what you mean, I remember once in my Catechism class when I was younger there was a girl who refused to attend after her parents got divorced because she moved in with her father and he wasn't religious.'

'Non-belief is a lesson that can be taught, even more quickly than the scriptures can be learned,' replied the older gentleman wearing white collar over his freshly ironed black shirt. 'May God have mercy on the children brought up in heathen households.'

'Thank you for the conversation, Father. I'll see you on Sunday.'

'Sunday it is. Tell your mother I said that I miss her attendance and look forward to seeing her on the holiday but wish she would come sooner.'

'Will do, Father. I try to get her to come more often, but she's been sick lately.'

'All the more reason to visit the house of the Lord.'

'Amen to that, Father, Amen to that.'

Recognizing the end of the conversation, and in an inexplicable hurry to get nowhere, Kyle stands up and continues his journey to the other side of the park, past the priest and his little green copies of the Bible. Avoiding eye contact, he walks a within a few feet of the clergyman but as no one else is passing, the older gentleman hones in on the young man. 'Good morning sir, would you like a copy of the New Testament?' Considering removing himself immediately from the situation rather than face an awkward conversation, Kyle freezes in place until he realizes that running away from a kindly priest is just as awkward as refusing the literature. 'No thank you.'

'Sir, the Lord would be much obliged if you would take a copy of His book. Maybe not today or tomorrow, but perhaps one day you'll feel the need to open it up to find some advice, compassion, or truth.'

From over Kyle's right shoulder comes a voice. 'Advice! Compassion! Truth! Father, leave the young man alone with your propaganda and your rhetoric. Leave him to think for himself.'

Recognizing a chance to fade into the more comfortable position of a bystander, Kyle slowly withdraws an arms length in order to watch and listen to the conversation from a more comfortable distance. The voice appears in the form of an eighteen year old that has ironically called Kyle young man. He is dressed in shabby clothes and looks as if he has not showered in weeks. Kyle can smell the alcohol on his breath and he finds himself wondering whether it's from the prior night, or this morning. Either way, the newcomer has been hitting the bottle hard. With him, he is carrying an armful of what appear to be newspapers. As if noticing Kyle's eyes on his papers, he reaches over and hands him one. 'Here, do some real reading. Get that garbage out of your head. My name is Aaron. Some friends and I put this together because we're sick of this asshole being the only one out here spreading their views.'

Looking to the priest for a reaction, Kyle finds only a peaceful blank face that holds no ill will towards the intruder. As if following Kyle's eyes, Aaron notices the lack of response by the priest. 'See, old man, people don't want your tired old sermons or your ridiculous stories of floods, plagues, and magic tricks. They don't want fantasy or leaps of faith. They want facts, reason, logic. Don't look at me like you don't know what I'm talking about. I heard you and that vile trash you were spewing to him when I walked up. Advice, compassion, truth? The Bible is hardly the place to look for advice. Sure, you'll find advice to any problem you have, but you can find advice sending you in either direction. This is how people are able to kill their children or their neighbors and hide under the guise of divine inspiration. If the Bible is a moral compass, it's the compass in your pocket while you're standing at the North Pole. Utterly useless.' Aaron stumbles a bit and has to grab Kyle's shoulder in order to avoid hitting the pavement. However, the near spill doesn't halt his thought process, and he continues. 'Compassion? That book doesn't teach compassion, it teaches lemmings. It teaches vengeance and revenge. God is a temperamental pubescent teenager. It teaches people to feel compassion if the preacher says to feel compassion. Sure, you feel compassion for the ill, but how about the unwed mother whose actions you're damning? How about compassion for the woman who has to make the unfathomably difficult decision of whether or not to give birth? How about compassion for Job when he is getting dicked over by God and Satan? Oh, and my favorite: truth. That book has nothing to offer anyone in regards to truth, sir. I was raised a good little Catholic. Our father who art in heaven, hallow be thy name. Yeah, I know all that nonsense. Thy kingdom come, thy will be done. What about *my* kingdom? What about *my* will? There's no truth in that book unless you believe people can live to be hundreds of years old and others can rise from the dead. People don't want myths, Father, they want reason and logic.'

With this final statement, Aaron draws in a deep breath and Kyle finds that the priest has been listening surprisingly carefully with his left eyebrow up inquisitively. 'If I may interject, you mentioned something about Job; what was that again?'

'Turn up your hearing aid old man. I asked whether we should have compassion for Job while he gets dicked over by God and Satan.'

'I believe that you should go back and re-read the book of Job. It has nothing to do with the power of God or Satan. It is an example of an ultimate faith in the Lord and payment that comes through belief in him.' As the old man finishes his thought, a second's worth of pity forms on his

27

face, but he quickly masks it as he fears it'll be taken as condescension.

'Listen, I'm not the one who needs to go back and re-read Job. You need to get your head out of your ass and look at what's happening! In the beginning of the book, God and Satan have a pissing match. God says, 'See how faithful Job is? You could ruin his life and he'll still worship me.' Satan starts ruining Job's life and God continues to allow progressively worse things to happen. Worst of all the dope continues to worship God and in the end, after having all of his things taken away and his life ruined, God appears on the scene to give him twice what he once had and praises Job for his faithfulness. Now, if that doesn't teach inaction and irresponsibility I don't know what does.'

Finally showing some slight irritation, the priest replies, 'I don't mean to preach, but you're focusing on the wrong part of the story. The point of the book of Job is to show-'

'Whoa, whoa. First off, you're a preacher so don't tell me that you don't mean to preach. Secondly, you read the story and focus on one thing and ignore the rest. I choose to focus on something else. Like I said, the Bible is a compilation of books where you can find any lesson you wish to learn, good or bad. Enough with the Catechism lesson.' Turning to Kyle, he continues, 'Read this stuff and

28

see if it doesn't make more sense than his theory that a loving god is testing people by allowing them to be tortured for years.' Aaron storms off in a huff, but not before giving one last look to, or perhaps through, the priest. He doesn't storm very far though, as he takes a seat on the bench Kyle has recently occupied. Perhaps he wishes to be within earshot of the priest as well.

Surprised at the scene he's just witnessed, Kyle sticks his chin to his chest and walks to the other side of the park. Before he is out of earshot, the priest calls to him, 'Son, think about this. You can believe or not believe. That is your decision and it doesn't concern me all that much. But ask yourself: do you really want to be as angry as the young man who we just witnessed? Who is more at peace? Him or me? Consider that. Good day.'

Without reflecting on much the priest had said, Kyle hurries out of the park to the main street where there is enough hustle and bustle to allow him to blend in comfortably. He sighs as he places one foot in front of the other. His thoughts begin to race regarding the conversation he'd just been privy to without any real validation of either point of view. He continues to walk, nudging his way between businessmen and wanders, with no concrete destination in mind. His mind is moving significantly faster than his feet. 'Why was that Aaron fellow so angry? Why didn't the preacher care that Aaron tore apart his God?

Why haven't I ever heard that interpretation of Job before?' All these questions race through his conscious and subconscious mind until it hits a brick wall. Kyle is immediately faced with one overwhelming question, 'What is most important: passion, truth, or peace of mind?'

Before having time to contemplate, or even fully realize the question, Kyle bumps into a middle-aged man who is struggling with the lock on the front of a tavern. 'Excuse me. I'm sorry, I'm a bit out of sorts today.'

'It's alright, no worries. This damn lock is always giving me hell. I bought this place a few months ago and the lock's been the bottom of my priority list.'

'Mind if I try?' The man with the salt-and-pepper hair quickly nods in assent, and before he can learn the young man's name, the door is opened.

'Wow, how'd you manage that?'

'I used to have a lock like this on the shed in my backyard. After a little practice, you get the hang of it.'

'Thanks, kid. Hey, this is a long shot, but you're not looking for a job, are you? I lost all the bartenders when I took over this place and I'm killing myself working every day and night.'

While Kyle doesn't believe in fate, destiny, or signs from above, occasionally things happen by chance that seem to fit right into the puzzle that is his life. His mind, still turning, travels back to the conversation he'd witnessed the park. 'The preacher this afternoon would have probably called this encounter a little help from God, but Aaron would have attributed it to chance or blind luck. Blind faith or blind luck,' Kyle thinks to himself, 'isn't there an option that's not blind?'

CHAPTER FOUR
THE DRUNKARD

After a few weeks of working at Jake's, Kyle has quickly learned the art of tending bar, and frequently works nights alone, giving his boss, Jake, the evening to himself. The young bartender is relentlessly grateful for the opportunity and constantly shows his appreciation by doing the job to the best of his ability. Jake, finally able to spend his nights at home with his television and weekends with his thirteen-year-old son, is enjoying his life much more and, with only sporadic help, has even begun to master the tricky front door lock. He repays Kyle's hard work by letting him bartend as often as he wishes, which Kyle takes advantage of. Soon he finds himself putting in full-time hours and making plenty more money than he had at the grocery store. For the first time in a few years, the fear of looming student loan debt around the corner holds no power over

Kyle as he puts a large portion of his tips every night into a savings account in order make the monthly payments which are fast approaching.

If there is one thing Kyle doesn't like about his new job, it's a handful of the patrons. While he has worked in customer service before and has become accustomed to the general public's inability to think before speaking, this is exaggerated exponentially when the same incredibly inept people are consuming intoxicating substances. In addition to their generally poor manors, arguments about how many drinks they've had, and the need to confess their life's problems, getting summoned over every few minutes by a drunk yelling 'Hey Kid! Get me another –' quickly grows old.

Over the past few weeks, Kyle has given his regulars appropriate nicknames. The Announcer is an older gentleman in his 60s who never shut up during any sporting event that is on the television. It's not that he ever has anything interesting or noteworthy to add, rather, it seems he is merely in love with his voice. To his right sits Chief. Chief is one of those guys who wants to be liked by everyone he meets, but he has a sarcastic way of saying 'hey there Chief' to every person he recognizes. It is painstakingly tolerated by most of the people who know him, but newcomers have the tendency to resist and ignore him. Always at the end of the bar is Big Fish – the guy who's always got a story that's one better than what you just told. If you stopped your nephew from falling into the lake, he dove in to get his and fought off a shark to save the young boy's life. Of course there was God who was appropriately named such because he always talked about the Good Ol' Days. Apparently things were much better fifty, sixty, and even seventy years ago. The cleverness of this nickname brought a proud smile to Kyle's face whenever he considered it. Big Bird was the only woman Kyle served regularly and one look at her explained her name. Lastly, there was Mickey the Mick who only drank Guinness and Kyle's most frequent patron, and most reserved character, the aptly named Drunkard.

The Drunkard sticks out as the most quiet of all his patrons, despite the fact that he drinks more than most. When more than a handful of people are in the bar, the only time he ever speaks is when he is spoken to or when he needs another beer. His voice is a conveyor belt, moving steadily regardless of what he is talking about. With it, his tone carries a sense of confidence not usually found in anyone, let alone a drunk surrounded by the class acts that frequent Jake's. While all the others in the bar take shots at each other, nobody ever says a bad word about the Drunkard and, likewise, he never badmouths anyone.

The Drunkard typically comes into the bar several times every week, already tipsy from downing wine bottles in the alley, and sits quietly at the end of the bar until Kyle brings him his draught beer. As if to thank him for the quick service, the old man is the only regular who doesn't complain about Kyle's inability to poor a perfect pint.

Late one night, the bar is as busy as Kyle has ever seen it due to some sporting event or another, and the Drunkard begins to pester Kyle about getting another drink. 'Hey Kid, get me another' he repeats constantly. Initially Kyle brushes him off and waits on the newly arrived, and nicely dressed, customers. Anyone who has worked in a bar for a few weeks quickly develops stereotypes for people in order to accurately determine the type of person who is likely to leave a good tip. Generally these rules are based on clothes, hair, what is ordered, and a category that is never admitted by servers, race. Despite their tendency to tip better on average, it's commonly known that the well-dressed, well-spoken crowd is usually the first to complain and diminish their tip due to a lack of perfect and immediate service.

'Hey Kid, get me another.' the old man continues to squawk.

'In a minute pal, can't you see I'm busy?' Coming to Jake's around two in the afternoon, and already a few bottles into his day, the old man has consumed more than he is accustomed to, and has pestered the young bartender much more than usual.

'C'mon, I'm a paying customer like the rest of these gator-shoed assholes. I'm here every day, the least you could do is get me another brew.' Getting more perturbed with every comment, Kyle resorts to ignoring him, but as can be expected this makes the drunken barfly more vile and unruly. 'Hey, Kid. Young fella, young fella, when I ask you to get me a beer, you're supposed to get me a goddamn beer. Now get your lazy ass over here and fill me up before I... I....' He wobbles just once and then *thud*.

Kyle thinks to himself that the old cliché of learning something new every day just might be proving itself true. He considers the new lesson quickly, 'The shaking of a fist on a stool, when you've been drinking for eight hours, may result in loss of balance and an inevitable fall.' Laughing mildly at the situation, but realizing the old man is causing a commotion, he decides to act as Jake had advised him whenever dealing with an unruly customer.

'Alright Buddy, you have two options. You get out of here and cool off for the night, or I call the cops and you cool off in a six-by-ten cell.' His threat falls on deaf ears. Growing frustrated due to the look on the faces of the well-dressed customers, he takes a slightly stronger tone. 'Hey, Pal, get out of here or I'm calling the cops. You hear me?'

Staggering to his feet, the old man mumbles 'Yeah yeah, cops, jail, I got you.' Placing a few wet dollar bills on the bar, he stumbles between the tables to the front door with the help of the bird-faced, equally inebriated regular. 'I'll see you tomorrow, alright, Kid? We'll talk about why you're kicking me out for n- why you're kicking me out for n- why you're giving me the boot for no damn reason.'

Worried that the professional patrons (that is, those who are professionals during the day as well as patrons of Jake's, as opposed to those who are patrons of a bar professionally) would tell their friends about the shady establishment they went to, Kyle apologizes to anyone who will give him the time of day. He attempts to convince his customers that the old timer has just had a bad day, has had a little too much to drink, and that this is not a frequent occurrence at Jake's. Realizing few are listening and an even small number seem to mind the disturbance, he hustles back to work giving people their third, fourth, or tenth drink when the grey-haired woman who helped the Drunkard out of the bar stumbles back in and sits in her usual beat-up seat.

'Thanks for your help in getting him out of here.' Kyle half-heartedly tells Big Bird as he places a bottle in front of her. 'That one's on the house.'

'Oh, it's no problem pumpkin, LT just had a little too much to drink tonight. In fact, I don't think I've ever seen him that drunk before. He always drinks and drinks and it never gets to him. Is there a full moon out?'

This reminds the young bartender of his high school and college days when his friends would blame alcohol for their actions every weekend. Thinking as much about his ex-friends as he is about the Drunkard, what Kyle wants to say to her is, 'People always do their damnedest in making excuses for their actions when they don't conform to their character. What they always seem to lose sight of is that it's their history of actions that create their perceived character, and an action outside that habit doesn't mean they're not acting like themselves, it just means their acting different than expected. No excuse is necessary and no excuse is sufficient. Some days people are fantastic, some days they're assholes. Some days people know when to cut themselves off, some days they drink too much. *C'est la vie.*' But he hastily reminds himself that nobody wants to listen to his lectures, especially in this place, and settles for 'Thanks again.'

The following evening, the old man who finally has a name, LT, slowly meanders back into his second home. He struggles to make it through the doorway with his tail between his legs. He immediately approaches Kyle and apologizes for his actions the prior night. To Kyle's surprise, LT offers no explanation or excuse as to why he acted the way he did. In fact, he doesn't even say that he'd had too much to drink. He merely looks the bartender in the eye and says, 'Hey Kid, I'm sorry for last night. I shouldn't have acted the way I did. I hope that you throwing me out wasn't a permanent decision. And I hope those folks tipped you well after seeing what you have to put up with.' He knocks on the bar at the not-so-clever jab at himself and winks at Kyle in hopes that he isn't the type of person to hold a grudge. Luckily, for the both of them, Kyle isn't.

Surprised by the man's acceptance of his dishonorable actions, Kyle grabs a mug and fills it with a medium grade beer. 'No hard feelings old timer, here's one on the house.' Kyle has no restraint in making the decision to buy one for LT after how well he made out the prior night. Thanks to the drunken buffoonery of this man, he had several of the well-dressed customers tell him that he'd handled it well and that he deserved to make more money than he does to put up with scenes of that sort. Graciously, Kyle accepted their tips, which helped him to make more money in a few hours than he usually did in an entire shift. Whether it is the tips or the way LT takes responsibility for his actions, Kyle begins to feel an immediate kinship with the old Drunkard.

Behind Kyle, on the all-day news channel, a young brunette reporter in a fashionable business suit explains the recent gubernatorial election in some random area of the country that has no significance to either person in the bar. The reporter explains that the election would have to be decided by the courts because of all the issues regarding vote counting, voter intimidation, and the issue of late absentee ballots. A long-time proponent of the abolition of the two-party system, and therefore a perpetually frustrated non-voter, Kyle scoffs at the battle between the equally contemptible candidates and switches the television to the all-day sports channel.

Still considering the political battle, LT blurts out a thought without concern with whether the bartender will be interested. Elderly people have a tendency to assume they're inherently fascinating. It's either that, or desperation breeds an attitude where people are lonely enough that finding a friend is more important than the possibility of boring someone. 'Ya know, Kid, I've always felt that if you want to govern people, you have to place yourself below them,' he gives a little wink before continuing, 'and if that's the case, shit, I should be president of the world by now, don't ya think?' With a smile that only a drunk old man missing three of his front teeth can pull off, he takes his glass of beer to a table in the corner where he sits for a few hours, slowly sipping the unusually delicious beer that for once actually has the flavor of hops and barley.

Kyle turns his head to the television in order to watch the top plays from the night before only to glance back to take a look at the old man. Recalling LT's comment about government, he thinks to himself 'That was either the smartest or stupidest thing I've ever heard in my life.' Watching the old man enjoy his beer for a minute, Kyle smiles before turning back to find he's missed the top two plays. He cuts the power on the television set, grabs a wet rag from a suds-filled bucket, begins washing the counter and barstools, and decides that he would finally cast a vote if the Drunkard were on the ballot.

CHAPTER FIVE
JUSTICE AND TRUTH

The leaves are swirling in a pattern that is reminiscent of a constellation whose name is not nearly as important as the beauty it portrays. The clichés of a fall morning tend to mention the fog rising, the bitter chill on unsuspecting individuals who are trying to cling to the memory of the fading summer months, or perhaps the distant sound of birds chirping one last time before they migrate south in anticipation of the cold days ahead. Today is nothing of the sort. It's a surprisingly sunny fall morning lacking entirely of fog and noise. Perhaps Kyle has beaten the birds in waking this morning. Perhaps they're enjoying the silence together. The sun is shining on Kyle's face and the wind is taking its toll on his cheeks as he walks east down a small road lined with trees that overhang the street.

Without anything of significance on his mind, other than the increasing sense of loneliness and general lack of a direction to his life, Kyle sets out for a walk this Tuesday in hopes of finding some inspiration. This particular cold morning, Kyle finds himself thinking of the brilliant writers he grew up reading, 'Dostoyevsky was locked up as a political prisoner, Thoreau lived off someone else's land, Bukowski lived off of beer and motel rooms; what has been so special about my boring middle class upbringing that will lend itself to a story?' Rather than accepting this and working towards a goal, Kyle keeps small bits of stories in his head while waiting for something to happen. One can easily be fooled into wasting a lifetime waiting for something to happen. This procrastination is the road to the death of the human spirit. If one travels down the path for too long, one loses their bearings and can no longer get back to a path of productive creativity. Luckily, it is not too late for the young man knifing through the cold air this morning.

On this particular morning, Kyle follows a path through the trees until he reaches a park just outside the distance he frequently walks. He steps on the grass delicately as though afraid to disturb slumbering ants. He whistles to himself as he waltzes through the meadow-like outfield of the little league baseball diamond. He loosens the scarf around his neck and removes his hat and gloves. If nothing else, he's going to take this time to actually feel something. 'Whether pain from the biting wind, or warmth from the sun, this is no time for shields.' While he meanders home after a few minutes in the lonely park, he remembers his years in school and considers the life his classmates are currently living. Granted, Kyle has no real solid plan but he knows he would not be happy living in a world of doing what is best for a client rather than doing what is inherently right. He was and is willing to sacrifice stability in order to distance himself from a system in which the poor are unevenly treated due to their inability to afford proper counsel. Until now, the thought has escaped him as to how he is going to make his mark on the world. There is little or no doubt that he has something to say, it is just a matter of learning how to properly find one's voice. Surely he is not going to make a difference by making drunks drunker or telling the world where they can find toilet paper, cologne, wine, cookies, or the magazine rack.

All this time his plan has been to live the kind of life he wants to live, not the kind of life people expect him to live. This morning he is tortured with the question of whether his current situation is really the life he had in mind. Tending bar for the dregs of society is not exactly the life he has been hoping for. Kyle claims a desire to experience the gamut of human emotions and experiences, but to what end? For what purpose?

These thoughts race through his mind as he approaches his apartment door. To his surprise he notices a tiny piece of paper hanging out of the third mailbox from the right, which happens to have his last name on it. Not remembering the last time his mail was checked, he takes out his key and retrieves the small white envelope. Based on the handwriting and the quilt stamp, without looking at the return address, Kyle knows this is a letter from his mother. This seemingly minor incident forces Kyle to recollect the last time he has talked to a member of his family. Well aware that it has been more than a month or two, he feels a pang of guilt that is quickly overshadowed by curiosity of the contents of the letter. Knowing his family must have got his address from one of the few friends who he keeps sporadic contact with, Kyle forces himself to suppress rising anger at his big-mouthed friends. He hurries to his room anticipating a response to the correspondence he sent all those months ago, but is disappointed when he rips open the envelope to find only a short note in his mother's neat handwriting.

> *Kyle,*
> *No need for silly formalities. I've tried to call and email over the past few weeks but have been unable to reach you. You can't imagine the trouble I went through to find*

your address. Aunt Joyce is sick. Come home and see her before it's too late. Today they put her in hospice and only expect her to hold on a few more days. Please come home as soon as you can.

With Love,
Mom

It seems rather silly that his mother has acted as if he lives a few thousand miles away. It seems that's how it always is with mothers; whether a few dozen, a few hundred, or a few thousand miles, when the children leave it's as if they are light-years away. She could have just as easily hopped on the expressway and been to his apartment in less than a few hours, but this approach is most likely better for everyone involved. Reflecting on the letter, Kyle thinks, 'Awkward situations and conversations are much easier to have over text rather than actual conversation. There's no need to hide or feign emotion when writing; it's as if you can safely assume the reader will interject his or her emotion.' Sighing, Kyle recalls how his entire life people have told him he thinks too much.

After giving the letter a quick twice-over, and grabbing some food from his refrigerator, Kyle walks down the busy morning street in what can only be described as a

47

dense fog of the brain. His mind is clouded with ideas, worries, and thoughts about the information he has just received. However, it is as if this cloud has no weight to actually effect this morning's constitution. Nothing is going to ruin the gorgeous morning that is unfolding before him. He hasn't talked to his family in months and surely most people would find it important to pay last respects to his beloved aunt. However, for some unknown reason, Kyle feels entirely detached from the familial relationships. It isn't as if a relative is hopelessly ill, but rather as if a random stranger is on their deathbed. Pondering these thoughts, Kyle slowly makes his way to Jake's, unlocks the door, and begins setting up for the early afternoon rush.

He plays the stereo loud and begins taking down chairs and wiping tables when he hears the jingle of the front door. Without looking up he shouts, 'Sorry, we don't open for another 20 minutes.'

'You sure you don't want some company or a hand with those chairs?' a familiar voice yells back over the music. Kyle turns to see LT standing with the most sober demeanor he has ever seen the Drunkard maintain. Knowing he won't be much of an inconvenience, the young bartender tells him to grab a seat, relax and not to worry about the chairs. Not one to argue, LT takes a seat, watches Kyle work, and immediately notices an unusually tense seriousness to the face of the young bartender. 'What's on your mind this morning, Kid?'

'What was that?' Kyle half-yells over the music. Aware they will not be able to converse in this manner he sets down his rag and walks over to the stereo to adjust the volume knob. Usually of a tight-lipped nature, Kyle finds himself surprisingly eager to air his thoughts to someone. A personal epiphany passes through his mind 'Maybe it's finally catching up to me that I have no real friends.' He dismisses the thought as quickly as it arrives.

'I said, what's on your mind this morning, Kid? You seem a little preoccupied.'

'Well, if you honestly want to know, I just got a letter from my family telling me to come home as we're soon going to have a death in the family.'

'Oh, well I'm sorry to hear that Kid. So were you close to 'em?'

'No, no, it's not like that. It's my aunt. I'm not all that concerned with her, but I had planned to cut my family out of my life for some time while I sort of find my own life.'

'Well it sounds like your family needs you.'

'That's just the problem' he replies, slightly irritated that the old man doesn't intuit what he hasn't yet said. 'I know that my family wants to see me, but I just don't think I want to see them.'

'Well, something awfully bad must have happened for you to cut your family out like that.'

'Not really. It's just...' Trying to collect his thoughts he sits for a minute with his eyes closed. 'It's just that the life that they wanted to give me, which is an entirely decent life, is not the life I want. They want me to be something that I don't care to be and they think that if I'm not, quote, successful, that I'm a failure.'

'Sounds like most families. My wife used to tell me that I was a lousy drunk of a bum that would never amount to anything, but look at me now' the old man recalls with a smile that isn't returned. Recognizing that humor may not be the appropriate approach, he puts on a serious face and continues, 'Ya know, Kid, I don't know what they expect of you or what you expect of yourself, but the only thing that matters is your relationship to yourself. The thing is, most people care about whether they have a relationship with their families, so in doing what their families want, they're working towards something they value. I suppose if you're not worried about your relationship with your family.... The point is that you're happy, aren't you?'

'See, at least someone understands. They'll just continue to ask me when I'm going to be a lawyer and whether I've applied to any big law firms, but they just don't understand that I'm not going to be a lawyer just because I did the schooling for it. Just because you have hands like a surgeon doesn't mean that you'll be happy as a surgeon.' LT keeps quiet, hoping the young bartender will continue, which he does as the emotion creeps up and the fog lifts. 'It's this legal system that I can't stand. It's lawyers that I can't stand. So why in the world should I be a part of it? For money? What a lousy reason to do anything.'

'Surely not all lawyers are bad, Kid. If it wasn't for a few of those suits, my ex old lady would still be attached to me.'

'Yeah, there's good work to be done out there, but even good work is ruined by a broken system. It's this adversarial garbage that you constantly have to be working for the benefit of your client. What happened to Truth and Justice. Those were the reasons I went to law school, but the only thing that I realized is that you'll find Truth and Justice in a court room as soon as you'll find a quadriplegic playing the fiddle.'

'Heh. Nice. I once saw a guy play guitar with his feet. It was incredible.' He laughs to himself, visualizing the scene he'd once witnessed, 'He was terrible.'

Frustrated at the anecdote, Kyle continues, slightly louder than before, 'Well, ya know, maybe somewhere there's someone that can play like mad without limbs somehow, but I can tell you that it wouldn't be pretty, and it wouldn't be easy, and people can't handle things that aren't pretty or easy. It's just, the system is broken beyond repair and I've come to terms with the fact that I want no part of that system. Sure, I learned some good things in school about my rights, but that's all I'm taking away from law school. I don't even have a diploma to show for it and I'm absolutely fine with that.'

'So you didn't stick it out?'

'No, I stuck it out and graduated. I just burned the diploma and sent a picture of it to my mother. Now that I think of it, it was a pretty spiteful thing to do, but what can I say? It accurately reflected my feelings and I'd do it again if I had the chance.'

'You do realize that your job doesn't have to define you, right? I mean, look at me, I'm a professional drunk but that's not all there is to me. I like taking walks in the early morning before the booze runs out of my system and eating a Pay Day in complete silence.'

'Yeah, I know that my job doesn't have to define me, but my actions do define me and if I'm working for something that I don't believe in I'll only grow to hate myself for it.'

'A man with principles, I can respect that. Say, man with principles, do you mind breaking one of those instrumentalities of the system that you loathe so much?' Kyle looks at the old man, perplexed. 'Gimmie a beer Kid. I know you're not allowed to serve for another, oh, eight minutes, but you said yourself that you won't find Justice and Truth in a court room.'

Kyle continues the conversation as he fills a beer stein from the tap, 'I'm not looking for Justice and Truth in a bar either, old man. I'm just looking to make enough bank to scrape by until I figure out what I want out of my life.'

'Do tell. What do you want with your life?'

'Hell if I know. Hell if I'll ever figure it out, but I'm going to live *my* life *my* way until I figure it out.' Kyle blurts out, irritated, as he sets down the beer in front of the balding man. An ounce spills over the edge and Kyle watches LT's eyes follow the wasted booze. Their discussion begins to sounds like a conversation Kyle might encounter if he goes home, and the young man is grateful to have practice with such a non-judgmental character.

As silence falls over the two, Kyle goes back to setting up the bar for opening in a hurry as he notices that it's already a few minutes after eleven and the lunch rush will be arriving soon.

'So what do you think? Think I should go home even though I don't really want to?' Kyle asks, hoping to get something to push him in one direction or the other.

'Well, if you're worried about your family getting on your case about not being what they call successful, ask them this: what's actually more destructive, success or failure?' Kyle looks at him rather cross-eyed, unsure of exactly what that will accomplish and after taking a sip of his beer the old man continues, 'And while they're pondering that, you can jump out a window and hurry back to this gold-mine of salvation.' With a bright gap-toothed smile, the old man stretches his arms out as if the entire establishment were on display as he finishes his thought, 'this gold mine-mine of salvation, and beacon of Justice and Truth.'

The bell rings and customers from the local office buildings begin to enter looking for a bite to eat and a little drink to take the edge off before going back to their monotonous and utterly dull lives.

CHAPTER SIX
ORIGINS OF THE DRUNKARD

Due to the fact that Kyle is so highly valuing the advice of his favorite patron, it has become necessary to pause the story for a moment so that there can be a brief account of the history of LT, the Drunkard.

Since the time of his birth, LT was frequently frowned upon by family and friends because of his simplistic thought and ineffable lack of motivation to make anything of his life. His father and mother were affluent professionals in the fields of scientific research and psychological research, respectively. Their home was s shrine of technical books, which were organized by subject area, then kept in strict alphabetical order, by author. While his family taught him to read at an early age and impressed on him the importance of attaining outstanding grades in school, LT quickly found a desire to rebel against the wishes of his parents by refusing to obtain more than scarcely passing marks. Chastised by his parents on a regular basis for his sub-par performance, LT grew resentful of their way of life. The family hired a tutor who was invariably frustrated and angered by the child's ability to house absolutely no interest in the subjects being taught, or in pleasing his parents. At the age of fifteen, LT ran away from his parents and their house of books never to see them again. He obtained a job in a factory painting cans for a pittance and refused any possibility of promotion or extra responsibility. He slept in alleyways and spent his money on food and books, which he read then gave away. Early on, he learned that by not desiring things that most people cherish, they flocked to him. Almost immediately, a young man his age who worked at the same factory invited LT to stay with him in a lodging house owned by an elderly woman who cooked them a bountiful breakfast each morning. The boys became the best of friends, sharing a room, clothes, food, and sometimes women. LT neither saved money nor considered where his next meal would come from. At the ripe age of seventeen, LT had learned the ability to live day-by-day and minute-by-minute. While such shortsightedness may cause tribulations for many people, when an individual is not concerned with anything more than eating their next meal, whether it be a few hours of a few days away, there is little to fear. Whether it was promotions, extra hours, friends, or women, he strove for none but was constantly blindsided by an overabundance.

At the age of nineteen, after several years of working at the factory, LT suddenly began to find satisfaction in taverns, and more importantly in the power of alcohol. Rather than stuffing his small bag with apples, bread, and a new book every week after work, he slunk into a seat in a nearby tavern and drank away his hard-earned money. To many people, the attraction of alcohol was to forget their day, their boss, their worries, their problems, but LT implored his comrades that without any real problems, alcohol was merely a way to embrace life in all of its forms. He claimed the intoxicant was neither necessary nor particularly helpful to any man. If nothing else, it kept him warm on cold nights and a chilled beer kept him cool on balmy summer afternoons.

While LT may have told his friends that there was no reason for his turning to alcohol, this couldn't be further from the truth. Such powerful personas have the tendency to hide small truths from themselves. In doing so, they're able to maintain an honest demeanor while they lie to themselves and others regarding their motivations. Despite the fact that LT told himself and his friends nothing drove him to take his first drink, it occurred because of a very specific circumstance.

Late one Saturday night, the young factory worker was walking home from work with his pockets lined with his week's earnings. He was internally rejoicing in the thought of buying a new copy of Goethe's *Faust* because his had been read to the point of ripped pages and smeared ink. His roommate of several years had recently switched to a morning shift, so the young man found himself walking through the city alone in the dark. As he approached a small intersection in his neighborhood, he saw a piece of trash dancing with the wind in the middle of the street. He thought it sad that any second now the car a block away would come to interrupt the beautiful dance. However, as he approached closer, he found that it was not a piece of trash dancing with the wind, but a bird struggling to fly, violently flopping around the intersection. Without hesitation, he ran out into the street causing the car to slam on its brakes and honk the horn at him as he picked up the bird and rushed back to the sidewalk.

Carrying the beast close to his chest, he told it that it was beautiful and was going to be just fine. He couldn't find any reason why it was in such pain, but still cradled it for a few minutes before its continual fighting allowed it to break free of his hands. As he watched the beautiful bird rise from his grasp, he displayed the pure smile of a child until he saw the bird plummet back into the pavement from ten or twelve feet above the hot road. Rushing back into the street, he again saved the poor thing from being hit by a car and carried it off to the sidewalk. As he held it close to him, he felt the bird take a deep breath, then another, then go limp.

Never had anyone felt so close to life and death in one instantaneous moment as LT did standing on the side of the road with the dead bird in his hands. With tears streaming down his cold motionless face, he walked to a nearby park and buried the beautiful breathless beast below a tree, all the while apologizing for letting him go, and for holding him too tight.

Whether or not it surfaced consciously is unknown, but at that point, LT became aware with his entire being of the inevitability of death and the utter uselessness of struggling against life. He found truth in the idea that life and death are rivers, and when one falls in, one must work with the current, not against it. To work against it is futile, but to submit yourself to it completely is divine.

It was that evening that LT walked into a tavern for the first time and asked for a drink; any drink. It was that evening that LT found peace of mind in the bottom of a large glass. Sitting at the bar, the young man was determined to let life and death come to him as they would and not to fight against them.

For the next fifty years, LT would allow jobs, cities, and friends to come and go without so much as batting an eye. It wasn't that he never felt attached to particular jobs, places, or people, but that he accepted the circumstances he found himself in. Call him a lousy drunkard or a useless waste of space if you will, but recognize that LT is a man with no regrets; a mindset that most people aspire to.

CHAPTER SEVEN
FLEETING INSPIRATION

After his lengthy conversation with LT regarding the potential visit home to see his sick aunt, Kyle has decided to give in to his mother's request, if only for a day, and his boss acquiesces without a second thought. Kyle packs and is on the train the following day.

In the early evening, Kyle marches up the drive to be received by his family who are out on the porch watching dusk roll in. Walking up to the familiar house, Kyle fends off memories of his childhood that come flooding back. His family greets him with hugs and guilt trips about his lack of contact with them and he brushes this off as an expected confrontation that is better suited for a lack of response. Immediately, they catch him up with the situation by informing him that he is too late and his aunt has passed away. Not feeling much, Kyle feigns despondency and quickly retreats to the comfort of the sofa downstairs to get some rest. This rest lasts until the following day when his mother wakes him and tells that the funeral service is to begin in an hour.

Playing the part of the devastated relative, Kyle keeps to himself and decides to walk the several miles to the funeral home both to enjoy the brisk morning, and to have some time to himself. On his walk he considers how death has never greatly affected him. Only a select few people have died that he was ever remotely close to and it has never produced much emotion in him save for frustration with everyone else's outcries and seemingly overdramatic reactions. It was realized and accepted long ago, after the death of a classmate, that people do not grieve for the deceased, but rather for themselves. 'But some people feel sympathy or empathy for the grieving family,' he thinks to himself and quickly comes to the conclusion that these feelings seem wasted emotions.

His mind continues to turn as the sun beats on his brow while the cold autumn air peppers his face. 'I don't know when I got so cold and dead inside. I remember the days when the thought of a death instilled in me a hint of curiosity, but supreme despondence and unshakable fear. I remember growing up and being brought to tears by a film or a record, but in the past few years it's as if my emotions have gone numb. As if part of my brain has been shorted out due to over-activity. As if we, as humans, are all given an allotment of tears and emotional pain for our lifetime and some of use them as infants, children, or throughout our lives but I used most of mine in my teenage and young adult years. My tears have run out. The well is dry.'

Walking up the entrance to the funeral home he sees how many cars are parked in the lot and immediately regrets his decision to come home. As he watches people walk into the funeral home in their black suits and inexpressibly colorless faces and clothing, he realizes that he has neglected to bring socially appropriate attire. For the remainder of the day, the *wish wish* of his corduroy trousers would mock him, reminding him of this oversight. After removing his jacket and scarf, the bare arms protruding from his plain navy t-shirt and the scruffy short beard that have been growing on his face for some time now will force him to be the outcast of the occasion; a position he finds himself invariably comfortable with. Kyle finds himself preparing to deal with his mother's comments about his lack of respect. 'As if Aunt Joyce can see me or would care about my clothes.' He would have to bite his tongue.

Slowly entering the funeral home he is greeted with smiles and looks of sorrow. It seems that people are curious and excited to see him, but obviously and understandably not under this circumstance. Like a magnet, his eyes are drawn to the eyes of others but as they look up, the north pole meets the south and they immediately shy away from the confrontation.

Within an hour he has extended family members and friends of the family approaching him to inquire as to what he's doing with his life. However, due to the setting, every approach begins with one of two pitiful icebreakers. 'How are you holding up?' or 'I'm so sorry for your loss.' It's as if in the obituary and the emails that were sent out regarding the funeral there was a notice informing everyone to say one of these two ridiculous statements. Either approach leaves Kyle with nothing to respond so he merely stands silently until the awkwardness fades and the individual commences the obligatory chatting. Soon the dreaded inquiry begins: 'So, when are you done with law school? Oh, you're done. What are you doing now?' 'Where are you working?' 'Going to work at a big fancy bankruptcy law firm?' 'Going to work at a big fancy real estate law firm?' 'Going to work at a big fancy patent law firm?' 'I have a friend who is a lawyer named Brian Kessel, do you know him?' 'Do you have a card? I might need a lawyer sometime soon.' 'So I have a legal question....' The only effect each of these has is to cause the glossing over the young man's eyes and the resurgence of an intense and unequivocal feeling of regret. Generally he tells people he doesn't know what he is going to do but that currently he is happy tending bar and that he doesn't feel drawn to the legal profession. Not being the answer people expect, they cut the confrontation short.

As soon as there is a lull in the line to discuss legal matters with him, Kyle heads outside for fresh air and doesn't return to the funeral home or to what used to be his house. It is only fifteen and a half miles to the train station and it is a good day for a walk, although the bare arms under his jacket start to get chilly as the sun begins to set. Winter is beginning to set in. A funny thing happens while he is wandering down the busy streets. For the first time in a long time, Kyle starts to think about his future. Perhaps the funeral is having an effect on him, but he is much too stubborn to admit it. As he sits on the train to return home, Kyle removes the notebook from his bag and begins to make a list:

Plant a tree as a seedling and help it grow.
Plant a garden and grow my own vegetables/fruits for a year.
Hitchhike.
Paint a self-portrait.
Fast for a month.
Write a song.
Learn a magic trick.
Write a book.

Looking at the list a new feeling resonates throughout his body. It's as if his entire being is vibrating at the same rate. Warmth comes over him as he realizes what most of these goals mean. Planting, painting, singing, and writing. The least common denominator of these is the act of creation. Perhaps this is the hole that has been feeling so hollow as of late. The hole he has attempted to fill with women or booze on occasion. Perhaps this is the object to fill it: creation. While matter cannot be created or destroyed, ideas can, and to create in this sense is divine. An act of creation is an act of god that no soul, other than the creator, can ever fully comprehend. This, Kyle decides, is going to be the purpose, for now, to his life. To leave a footprint behind him wherever he goes, regardless of when he dies.

During the trip back to his apartment he considers where to start with his newfound list of life goals. He's run out of paints in the last few months and replenishing his supplies will require a tidy sum of money, and a song requires a musical instrument and knowledge of that instrument. Planting requires at least a minimum amount of land, which Kyle doesn't have. Writing requires a computer or a pen and a notebook, all of which Kyle has. The young man is determined to begin that night, but what is there to write about?

No story comes to mind, but this is a moot point as Kyle's bed is met with his body as soon as he walks in the door and, exhausted, he immediately falls asleep to find himself living in dreams of vibrant paintings and the most beautiful songs. The next afternoon Kyle wakes up and leaves without any contemplation of the story he plans on writing. Considering the night before, he is deeply frustrated and disappointed with his inability to stay motivated. Inspiration came and left due to his desire to sleep surpassing his desire to act on inspiration. As he commutes to work on foot, he talks quietly to himself. Shaking his fists next to his hips, he begins, 'The problem with inspiration is that it's just that: Inspiration. If someone is inspired, moved, or touched by something a person says or does, it generally has no effect other than to touch them. While this connection is what so many artists strive for, is it really anything?

'The problem with inspiration is that it's just that: Inspiration. How many people see a work of art, a film, hear a piece of music and say to themselves 'Wow, I wish I could do that. It's beautiful.' The individual is inspired, but are they really any better off because of it? Is the world any better off because of it? An effective affect would be something like 'Wow, that's beautiful. One day I'm going to create something with that much passion. I'll try today. I'll try right now.' Inspiration is nothing without some follow-through or action. We can inspire people or be inspired all day long but have not made a *significant* difference in the world unless someone acts on that inspiration.

'The problem with inspiration is that it's just that: Inspiration. We need to stop searching for inspiration as a lonesome trait. Search for inspiration partnering with action. This, my friends, is worth attaining.' Kyle finishes with a smile as he reaches Jake's bar. Jake is surprised to find the young man home so quickly and decides to leave and let Kyle take over for the remainder of the day.

While this pep talk feels to Kyle like the motivation he needs to begin acting on his new view of life, it is merely fleeting, transitory inspiration. At work he gets caught up in the job and the patrons. Without coupling his new mindset with immediate action, Kyle's urgency and excitement quickly fade. While his life goals remain posted on the wall in front of his bed, they quickly transform from an inspiring list to an unnoticed scrap of paper that blends in with the white paint, and his life continues as it was before the funeral.

CHAPTER EIGHT
MAN OF THE MOMENT

Like many times in his life, after being temporarily inspired, Kyle resumes the daily grind, forgetting completely his list of things to do before he dies. He continues serving drinks to businessmen in the afternoon, college kids at night, and hopeless walking disasters all day, every day. The bell rings at two o'clock in the afternoon and the sunlight through the windows creates the illusion that the dirty clothes crawl into the bar of their own volition. The granite face of an overworked man sits down, directly in front of the bartender, and promptly orders a whiskey and a bottle of cheap beer. Attempting to feel out the newcomer, Kyle hands him the drinks and asks with a smirk, 'Hey buddy, what are you doing wearing your church clothes into the bar on a Tuesday?' The man looks not one bit amused at this seemingly low blow at his attire. Immediately recognizing the worm isn't about to be bit,

Kyle continues, 'Your church clothes, man. They look awfully holey to me.' Whether it is the first sip of booze or the horrible attempt at humor that reminds the man of his grandfather, the granite face begins to crack and he smiles and thanks the bartender.

A few drinks later, the gentleman begins to open up to the young barkeep. 'Hey youngster, let me give you some advice.' Always entertained by such situations, Kyle brings an attentive ear to the man on the stool and stops cutting lemons in order to provide his full attention. 'You're a young guy still. Don't waste your life on thinking about tomorrow. Live every single day like it's your last.'

As always, the intoxicated sage is providing Kyle with what he believes to be invaluable advice. 'Listen, you look at me and see a drunk piece of shit, but last night man, you won't even believe what happened to me last night. So I'm at this dirty joint on the other side of town and I meet this lady at the bar. She looks like she's depressed as hell, she said she was going through a divorce or some shit, and after some drinks she lets me take her home and plow the shit out of her. Wait, wait, that's not the best part. So her roommate comes home while she's on top of me, ya know, giving it to me real good and her roommate hears us and comes in the room and man, you should have seen the tits on this woman. She had a rack like a moose. She walks in and we stop for a second and she sits on the bed and takes out a bag of blow and a straw. It was like she knew I was there and came prepared. Now I haven't messed with that shit for a few years, but I was due. So we all take a hit or two and she starts taking off her clothes and pushes off her friend and climbs on top and starts fucking me. It was wild man. Wild. Every guy's dream. If I had been worried about work in the morning or consequences of my actions I might not have gone home with her and look at what I would've missed out on.'

Kyle smiles and replies 'Sounds like you had one hell of a night.'

'Yeah man, but that's what I'm getting at. That's the point. It's not one hell of a *night*, it's one hell of a *life*. Every night I get fucked up and fucked. People have it wrong with that whole life-goal shit. Worry about today, every day, and you'll be better off for it. If you don't live in the moment, you never *really* live.'

Used to the rants of random people, Kyle isn't much phased by this particular series of comments and merely turns around to get the man another scotch, on the house. 'Here's one on me, man. Enjoy the moment for us both.'

Later that night in his apartment, Kyle is listening to music when the conversation from the afternoon resurfaces in a series of thoughts that he can't shake. Without consciously considering what he's doing, Kyle removes the

71

beat up journal he keeps in the top drawer of his desk. Not used all that frequently, the spine cracks as he opens to a clean page and, thinking of the gentleman he'd met in the afternoon, Kyle begins to write a letter to the man who he has dubbed, The Man Of The Moment.

Dear Mr. Moment,

I appreciate the story and life advice you provided me with this afternoon, but I've been doing some thinking about it. I've known plenty of your relatives throughout my twenty-plus years on this planet and while on some nights I feel that I could be a brother Moment, when I seriously consider your philosophy, I can't possibly resign myself to such a life.

I now recognize that every time in my life that I've turned to the 'live in the moment' mentality it's because I've been afraid of some possibility or lack of possibility in the future. This fear paralyzes me into thinking only of now and refuses to allow me any consideration for how my acts may affect anything outside the immediate future.

While I completely understand how you can live by the idea that if you live continuously for the moment you will come to love life for what it is rather than what it could be, I've found that if you ever plan on doing anything worth while in your life it will take dedication and hard work. If you're working today to put food on your dinner plate tonight, then you're working for something tangible, but nothing extraordinary. Some people are content with an ordinary life, but I recently came to terms with the fact that I want more out of my existence, and I want to give more to the world than my corpse when I die. Without getting on my soapbox too much, I feel that the world would benefit if more people would feel this way. Granted, everyone assumes that 'if everyone felt the same way I did, the world would be a better place,' but that doesn't necessarily preclude my thoughts from being valid. I want a lot out of my life, and with that I carry a lot of weight because you can only get out of life what you put in. However, I'm not afraid of it anymore because I've come to realize that this weight is all that matters in life and if I can carry it, I can do literally anything. The weight of the extraordinary man may be the heaviest weight to bear, but it is the most rewarding the only weight worth carrying.

I only hope to get this message to you before you ruin your life, or rather your moment. I feel that without having goals in life you're going to be constantly miserable. Granted, it's not the goals that matter, but the journey, and I feel that you're afraid of any journey so you resign yourself to booze, women, and drugs without concern for anything greater than your next high, but what you fail to acknowledge is that the greatest high you'll ever have is creating something worthwhile through hard work and dedication.

I hope that for your sake you'll reconsider your view on life and open yourself to the possibility of a high greater than that which you told me about this afternoon.

Loud Music And Evenings Alone,
Kyle

Kyle stops for a moment and rereads the letter. He considers whether anything good can come out of the sex, drugs, and rock and roll mentality. Realizing there's an important thought he's missed, a bit of an elephant in the room, he continues,

p.s. On a second reading of this letter, I realize that I forgot to mention that I don't think it's necessary to give up your current affinity towards drugs, sex, or women in order to give your life a higher purpose. In fact, they can be the greatest inspiration.

Kyle pushes back his chair and balances on its two legs while he looks at the neatly printed letter. He is glad to have written it. It seems to him that the more he writes, the more he is able to flesh out his thoughts. It's as if these ideas have been dormant in his head for as long as he can remember but have had no potential exit until now. As if putting a pen to a piece of paper opens a door, or at least a window big enough for the thought. With a sigh he puts down his pen, closes his notebook, and climbs into bed.

The sun peaks its way through the blinds in the small apartment and paints the room with sunlight, waking Kyle in the late morning. With birds singing and fog clinging to the windows, he looks at his desk and sees his notebook. He recalls, with a smile, the entry from the night before, and quickly acknowledges the release he felt after airing his conscience.

Kyle stretches and has a quick glass of orange juice before throwing on the same pair of corduroys from yesterday, another plain navy t-shirt and a suit coat. As he takes a step towards the door, the notebook catches his eye again. Without much thought, he rips out the pages he's recently penned, folds them carefully and places them into an envelope, writes 'Man Of The Moment' on the front and walks out of his apartment with the envelope stuffed in his satchel. Inspiration was finally coupled with the prospect of action.

CHAPTER NINE
THE RELENTLESSLY
HOPELESS ROMANTIC

It's an impossibly bitter morning where the breeze doesn't nip at your fingers and toes but bludgeons the back of your eyes. This results in an immediate headache united with the instantaneous regret of leaving the warm indoors. Kyle wakes early and leaves his apartment in order to take the long way to work, regardless of the unyielding weather. As he fights through the cold he passes grocers opening their stores, coffee and bagel shops with lines out the door, and dark lonely liquor stores. Kyle smiles or nods in respect to people he passes, and exchanges brief pleasantries with a few.

The beautifully youthful daughter of the Eighth Street grocer is helping her father lift crates of vegetables because the old man's back has been bothering him for the past few weeks. The widow with the fur coat is in line for coffee, impatiently tapping her foot, while playing with the exact change she has counted out for her daily double espresso latte with a shot of vanilla. The gentleman who owns the used bookstore is unlocking the front entrance when Kyle approaches. They exchange silent good morning greetings as Kyle follows him through the red wood door.

'Looking for anything particular today?' he asks, when Kyle begins to snoop through the new arrival section in front of the cash register.

'No sir, just looking.' After a minute of combing through the new arrivals, Kyle finds two of his favorite novels: an old edition of Blake's *The Marriage of Heaven and Hell* as well as several copies of Ayn Rand's *The Fountainhead*. A few years ago Kyle would have bought these with elation at the thought of giving two of his favorite works of art to close friends. Today he is saddened at the thought that he has nobody to give these wonderful gifts to, so he returns them to their respective spots and is about to leave when his eye catches a small but thick novel that has been accidentally placed backwards on the shelf. He removes the book from the shelf, and his curiosity turns to electricity as his eyes recognize the cover-art of an old man in a priest's robe, a young man wearing the garb of a wandering monk, and a beautiful woman in the arms of the wanderer. Kyle has found a copy of one of his favorite stories, which has been missing from his bookshelf since he had lent it to *her*. His frown at the thought of her turns to an inexorable smile at the memories of such a wonderful story. Excited, he takes the novel to the register and pulls a few wrinkled bills from his pocket. Kyle places the book on the counter and before turning around to assist him, the old man asks if he has found anything worthwhile. 'You could say that,' Kyle responds with a smile and the old man turns around to see the young man buying one of his favorite books.

'Wow, I haven't read this in ages. You're gonna love it.'

'Oh, I know I will. I used to have a copy but it's gone missing.' Kyle answers in his typical way of avoiding the full truth and having to share anything about his past. He hands over his crumpled bills and shovels the book into his bag before opening the bookstore door. As he reenters the cold, Kyle's heart is warm. Regardless of how far below zero the needle may drop, cold weather will never embitter a person with a warm heart.

Kyle arrives at Jake's an hour earlier than usual and takes a seat to look over his newly found prized possession. Rather than beginning to read it, he flips through the paperback attempting to find some of his favorite passages highlighted. The bartender is troubled to find that its previous owner has not taken the time to place a bracket around the most beautiful passages as Kyle has a habit of doing. Disappointed with this unknown person's lack of appreciation for what they were reading, Kyle places the book on the bar and begins to take chairs down from the tables. While he works, he can't keep his eye off of the beat-up cover. The woman on the front reminds him of *her*, of a less lonesome time. The slender figure on the book jacket hypnotizes him as he works carelessly and eventually drops one of the heavy chairs on his foot. He stifles a scream of pain just as there is a knock on the glass. Glad to have a distraction, he opens the door to find LT standing with a chattering grin that tells Kyle he wants a little something to warm up. 'Come on in, you look like a damned Eskimo out there.'

LT sits in his usual place at the end of the bar as Kyle fixes him with a beer and a shot of bourbon. LT immediately notices the book on the bar and walks over to see what it is. Not much of a reader anymore, LT yells to his young compatriot, 'Hey Kid, what's this *Narcissus and Goldmund* smut? You're a lot smarter than the romance novel crowd.'

'Romance novel? What are you talking about?' Looking over to see LT scrutinizing the picture on the front, Kyle understands the confusion, 'Yeah, I guess the cover looks cheesy, but that book changed my life. It's perfect. I just found it over at James' Books this morning.'

'So what's it about?' LT asks, half curious and half attempting to stifle the silence.

'Oh, it's about two friends who choose different lives. One decides to remain at school and become a priest and the other decides to go out and live the life of a lover and an artist.'

'So which one are you?'

'That's a good question. I always thought of myself as a Narcissus, living the life of the senses. But now that I think about it, I'm not much of an artist and ever since I moved to this town all I do is work and read.'

At that moment, as if someone somewhere didn't want them to finish their conversation, the bell rings and a man enters. Favoring his right leg, he limps his way to the counter. Despite the fact that the bar has twenty minutes before opening, Kyle is glad to have this interruption as he recognizes that he is about to divulge his thoughts to a stupid old drunk. The bartender snatches his book from LT's hands and asks the customer what he would like.

From that moment in the day the bell doesn't stop ringing and Kyle doesn't have a chance to sit and relax or to reflect on the fact that he hasn't thought about *her* since he left. He keeps his feet and his hands moving and is able to put aside the beating of his heart and the change in his breath that took place ever since he saw the picture on the front of the book. He finishes his shift at dusk, after staying a few hours to help Jake with the after-work crowd. Typically on Friday nights Kyle sticks around at the bar talking to Jake, avoiding going home. Tonight he feels an insatiable urge to relax in the comfort of his home. He exits the bar holding his bag close to him as if worried that someone will snatch his newly found, reacquired, treasure.

When Kyle gets home he sits at his desk and takes a deep breath before removing the book from his bag. He stares at the novel with anguish as he notices that the hands and feet of the woman on the cover are shaped just like hers. He will never forget the tiny fingers and seemingly oversized knuckles on her hands as he had felt them run over his skin so many times. With a shudder he opens the top drawer of his mahogany desk, takes out his notebook, and opens to a clean page. Before picking up his pen, he turns on the stereo to find one of his favorite pieces of music being performed.

Kaitlin,

It's been many months, and until today I've done an amazing job of avoiding thoughts of you. I've had my head in the sand for too long and it's time to face you through this page and explain myself as much as I can.

Almost a year ago I walked away from you without much of an explanation. I told you that I needed space and that you had done nothing wrong, and in that you must know I was being sincere.

The truth is, all my life I've been a relentlessly hopeless romantic. However, this has recently been increasingly detrimental to my existence rather than a blessing. Simply put, I feel that films and literature have warped my idea of Love into something entirely unattainable. In fact, I'm not even sure I believe in the idea of Love like most people do.

I don't know what to believe. Every relationship I've ever had, and every person that I've ever loved has been nothing more than a temporary fixation of all of my senses. Temporary being the key.

Before I left I became unavoidably bitter with Love and I need you to understand, again, that this is not because of anything you did or didn't do. You gave me space when I needed space and compassion when I needed compassion. However, I became what most people would consider selfish and started hating the idea of loving you or anyone else.

Inherent in the idea of love, it seems to me, is a sacrifice of the self. If you Love someone you should be willing to give all (or at least some) of yourself to that person. However, what I give to you, I lose for myself. At this point in my life I am not willing to give myself to anyone. Call me selfish, call me self-centered, but this is how I honestly feel and it would be unfair not to admit it to myself and to you.

I hate to use other people's words to describe my feelings, but I feel that it might help. D.H. Lawrence said something along the lines of 'the opposite of Love isn't Hate, the opposite of Love is individuality.' Now I'm not saying that I necessarily agree or disagree with him, but the truth of the matter is that I began to feel like that and started to resent you for it.

We're force-fed the idea that people immediately know that 'this is the one.' My problem with that is, and I hope you don't mind me saying this, that I fall madly in love with every person that I get romantic with. Every time I start dating I'm convinced that 'this is the one.' In fact, I even find myself falling in love with girls I see and neglect to talk to. So I've come to the conclusion that if I ever get married, that on my wedding day as well as six months and six years later, I'll be able to say that 'the day I met her I was convinced that she was the one,' but that it won't actually mean anything. It will be true, but will lack any real meaning.

This is probably the hardest thing to say: I'm afraid of Love. Throw out the trite clichés about Love, and you're still left with a terrifying concept of self-sacrifice and undying dedication. This is petrifying to anyone who desires individuality.

I guess all I'm trying to do is to explain my actions and myself as much as I can. I feel you deserve it and I feel that I've worked out some thoughts in the past few months, which you have a right to hear.

I'm not asking for anything, not even a response, which is why my address isn't included. I think you deserve an explanation. I hope this finds you well.

Selfishness and My Favorite Schubert Sonata,
Kyle

Luckily, the recent weather requires Kyle to keep a box of tissues on his desk, which he promptly uses to wipe the single tear that has welled up in his eye. The tear isn't due to the fact of writing a letter to his most recent love, but rather to the fact that he doesn't feel anything about it. It is a tear of numbness. Ever since the few months prior to walking away from the relationship, he has been overwhelmed with an utter lack of feeling. It's as if his most recent romantic spark blew the circuitry, which disabled him from attachment to any emotional or romantic feeling; as if his heart has been anesthetized by the needle of repeated disappointment; as if his fingertips no longer felt a beautiful human being below them, but merely the warm flesh of an animal. *Her* warm body had transformed entirely into *a* warm body, and this was when he realized it was time to leave.

As he shoves the letter into an envelope and places it in his bag on top of the letter to the Man of the Moment written the night before, he knows that she will never read it and is convinced that it is better this way. Kyle also knows that he will never again see the man who inspired him the night before, but nevertheless decides to keep both letters in his bag. He lies in bed drifting off to sleep and wonders where each of his muses currently is and what they're doing. He is sure the Man Of The Moment is either in a bed or a gutter somewhere. Possibly in the bed of a beautiful woman, but more than likely in the bed of a lowly depressed woman in her mid-forties, stained with alcohol and cocaine; or just as probable, a hospital bed. As for Kaitlin, she is doubtlessly sharing a bed with a man who actually deserves her. This thought causes no stirring in Kyle's heart or mind. The numbness he was experiencing has not subsided, but is strong and cold as ever. Luckily for Kyle, it is much easier to sleep in the cold.

CHAPTER TEN
THE COWARDLY CYNIC

'Hey Kid, remember that book you had in here the other day?' LT isn't quite drunk, but is closer than he usually gets and due to that, his voice carries through the rowdy and crowded bar early Saturday evening. 'Well, I was thinking that you seemed to clam up a bit when I was asking you about it. What was that all about?'

'LT, it's a little busy in here to have a heart to heart, and I didn't clam up, I just didn't feel like talking.' Kyle yells back as he fills drinks for young professionals and old college students. 'Don't worry about it man, I just had a bit of a rough morning yesterday.'

'Yeah, I can understand rough mornings.' He pauses, considering whether to press the issue, 'So what was bothering you, Kid?'

'Hey, I'm the bartender and you're the drunk. You're supposed to tell me your problems and I'm supposed to pretend that I care so that you stick around, drink more, and leave a nice tip.' Kyle retorts with a wink and a smile at the old man.

'Alright, alright, no more questions.' He takes the last sip of his now empty beer, 'Oh, except this: you know Maureen? She's usually in here on Tuesdays and Thursdays, gets a scotch and water, kinda looks like a bird.'

'Yeah, what about her?'

'Well, she wanted me to ask you, for her granddaughter, if you're available.'

'I'm not available for anything related to that crazy woman, that's for damn sure!'

Slowly everyone crowds around the two television sets and sits, silently watching, holding their breath as the big game comes to a close. Kyle takes this chance to fill LT's mug and takes a seat for the first time this evening. 'Man, these football weekends are killing me. I can hardly keep up. Jake's gonna have to get me some extra help.'

'Don't hold your breath. He can hardly afford to keep this place open let alone to hire another smartass kid like yourself.' After pausing a couple minutes during which they watch the televisions with the rest of the patrons, LT asks again about Big Bird's granddaughter. 'Really Kid, I hear her granddaughter is a knockout and a young guy like you shouldn't be running around without someone to squeeze by his side.'

'How do you know that I don't have someone to squeeze?' Realizing his defensive statement and tone won't get LT off his back, he confides in his friend, 'Trust me man, I can't handle a woman in my life right now. Too much work.'

Standing at the center of the bar without service for a minute and a half, a patron of his mid-forties feels the need to get the bartender's attention. Overhearing the conversation with the Drunkard, he speaks up. 'Hey man, women aren't worth the trouble anyway. They only good they're for is using their mouths to talk your ear off... or to remind you why you let them talk your ear off, if you know what I mean.'

'Hey buddy, sorry about not seeing you there. What can I get you?'

'If you really want to get me something, get me a new job man, or a new woman. Something's gotta change. If you can't manage that, then just get me a beer. At least that'll make me forget about my job and my wife.' Used to the random ranting of men going through midlife crises, Kyle places a beer on the bar and tells the patron to keep his head up, that things will get better. 'Yeah, you young kids have the world ahead of you, right? Keep your head up; what bullshit. The only time to keep your head up is when you're about to get the shit kicked out of you. At least go down with some pride.'

'With that attitude all you're ever gonna do is complain about life.' LT slurs into his nearly full beer, but it leaks into the conversation.

'Who the fuck are you to tell me what I'm going to do with my life, old man? Look at you. You're drunk as hell and not doing anything with yours. You're just as bad as them.' pointing to the crowd staring at the televisions, 'Those lemming assholes huddle around the set as if this game actually meant something and this bartender pretends to listen to people's problems so that he can make a few extra bucks. Bars are a microcosm of everything that is wrong with the world. Fake people and people with no priorities. I'm surrounded by assholes and people pretending not to be assholes which, naturally, makes them even bigger assholes.'

Ignoring this rant completely, Kyle asks the man if he wants another drink and promptly fills the glass. 'Hey kid, let me tell you something. If you ever want to do anything in life, don't trust other people. Other people will just bring you down and disappoint you. You have only one person you can trust in this world, and that's yourself.' With that, he slams the last of his drink, leaves four dollars and twenty-five cents on the counter and walks out without looking back.

'Just wonderful' Kyle thinks as he picks up the money, 'I listen to that guy rant for fifteen minutes and he gives me a whopping quarter for a tip. He tells me people are disappointments and assholes, but all he really shows me is that he's an asshole.' Getting back to their conversation, Kyle turns to LT, 'Alright, tell Maureen I've got a girlfriend of five years and a two year old baby girl at home and I wouldn't leave her for anything in the world. That should keep her and her granddaughter away from me.'

LT nods and after some thought says, 'I don't know what happened with you and your last girl, but I can tell you're not over it. Listen, if you realize that everything with women changes, all those romantic feelings, all that excitement, then there's nothing you'll try to hold on to. If you don't try to hold on to anything and just accept it, well, then she'll want nothing more than to hold on to you and you'll want nothing more than to oblige.' Kyle pretends he's not listening and continues to fill drinks of those celebrating or mourning the end of the football game.

For the third night in a row Kyle finishes his shift at the bar and goes home to his notebook. He wonders how long random people will continue to inspire him as he sits down to write a letter to the man he met tonight.

Mr. Cowardly Cynic,

Tonight at the bar you told me everything that is wrong with the world, and I appreciate that. However, you offered me no suggestions as to making the world a better place. It takes a Man to notice and point out problems with the world, but it takes a Great Man to cure those ills.

While I appreciate the fact that you can find flaws in anything and anyone, I can't help but wonder whether you can find beauty in just as much, or in anything at all.

You spoke of humanity as if it were some screwed up experiment in which it's too late to fix. Any scientist can recognize a flawed experiment, but only great scientists can suggest a better one.

Despite all this, your cynical attitude was not the most distressing part of our brief acquaintance. The most distressing part of our conversation was your complete and utter lack of passion or hope.

I meet plenty of drunk people in the bar who say that they're going to tell me something, however all they ever do is recount to me the sores that are open for everyone to see. You are just like all the others. Your cynicism makes you neither intelligent nor wise, but rather it provides the world with a perfect example of the term pitiful. I hope you can get your head out of the dark cloud where it currently resides and I hope you find some sort of passion in or for life. Passion and hope, even in seemingly silly things, will give you a life worth living.

I hope that we meet again so we can discuss your progress as well as mine because in watching you, I've become aware of a person that I wish to never become.

With Passion and Optimism,
Kyle

This third letter makes Kyle feel a way he hasn't felt with the other two. This epistle forces realizations about himself that he has never consciously acknowledged. Kyle immediately accepts and appreciates what writing offers him; a vehicle to not only express himself, but a vehicle to learn about and from himself.

With the third envelope in his bag, for the first time in as long a time as he can remember, Kyle decides to take a long walk before turning in for the night. While he has walked this neighborhood so many times before, this time he notices things he has never seen or really grasped. For the first time he observes how perfectly painted the house on the corner is and how imperfect and slanted their white fence in the backyard is. For the first time, Kyle perceives the abandoned house across the street and how the moonlight bounces off the front window. For the first time, Kyle notices how the streetlights allow him to see directly in to the living room of the ranch next to the abandoned house, where a young couple cuddles on the couch. For the first time, Kyle detects how sweet the freshly cut grass smells as it lays on the lawn in the courtyard and the way the flickering lights mounted to the side of his blood-red brick building cause shadows to dance on the sidewalk. For the first time, for no reason, Kyle smiles and sees beauty everywhere he looks.

CHAPTER ELEVEN
WHISTLING DIXIE

Following the night of beauty he's taken twenty-five years to realize, Kyle cannot manage to sleep but a few minutes. However, he finds this brief slumber to be more refreshing than any he has ever experienced. It isn't a matter of getting eight hours of sleep or sufficient REM sleep that makes one able to hop out of bed in the morning. The psychiatrists and sleep therapists have been feeding us lies for centuries and we've been swallowing so readily that our gag reflex is no longer existent. Sadly, this inability to distinguish good ideas from bad has infiltrated every area of our lives. Good sleep isn't a matter of exercise, staying hydrated or having the perfectly set temperature. In fact, it isn't even a warm body next to you that makes the first rays of sunshine in the early dawn bearable. The only condition for restful sleep is the knowledge, the assurance, that the world is a beautiful place, housed in a mind that has acquiesced to the idea of approaching life as a creator rather than a stander-by. It is knowledge of the power and possibilities that each day brings that makes the morning a relief rather than a burden. To those who work miserable jobs to pay for their miserable homes and overindulgent stuff for their miserable spouses, the morning is a reminder of the never-ending suffering that is life. For Kyle, this suffering is merely part of the life experience, but a severely overstated and unnecessary part at that.

While he struts down the sidewalks to work, Kyle finds himself humming and whistling, not just in his heart but also aloud for the whole world to hear. The people he passes glare at his unfathomable ability to be in such a swell mood, and are confounded to find that their dirty looks do nothing to shirk the young man's singing lips and singing soul.

As is beginning to happen frequently, Kyle's favorite regular is knocking on the door of Jake's twenty minutes before opening and the bartender yells that it is unlocked. The appearance of the morose-looking old man does nothing to halt the symphony within Kyle's chest or the symphony that is taking place through his lips. The Drunkard takes his seat at the end of the bar without saying a word and closes his eyes to listen to the young man's heartbeat through the sound waves exiting his lips. Most people can't whistle or hum a tune for anything, and while not exactly a world-class musician, this morning Kyle has the ability to throw his inhibitions to the wind and let his soul sing. It has long been true that passion will outdo technique eleven times out of ten.

Setting down a tall beer and a whisky in front of the smiling old gentleman, Kyle finds himself pouring out recollections of his previous night regarding the beauty and inspiration he discovered. He also finds himself mouthing words he had not even taken full grasp of. 'So last night I decided what I want to do.'

'Yeah? Well good for you, Kid. I'm happy for you.' The old man refuses to take the bait and ask for details. He is of the mindset that if the youthful bartender wishes to share his aspirations with him, nothing will alter that from happening. After a few seconds, the old man's wisdom becomes evident and Kyle begins to set forth his thoughts about life.

'See, I've been thinking a lot about it lately and while I recognize that this may be a fleeting thought, for now I feel the call of the pen. I want to write.' Refusing to allow anyone to stop the moving train that was his mind, Kyle continues. 'I know, I know. Everyone's going to tell me that this is childish and naive, but I don't care. This is what I want and nobody is going to talk me out of it. I got to thinking that the place I've found so much inspiration in the world is through other people's writings. I've more soul mates who died a hundred years ago and left me their footprint than I have people I feel I can relate with today. Last night, for the first time I saw just how beautiful the world is and if I could pass just a hint of that on to others....' He trails off from the monologue that has been stewing within him all morning and hurriedly begins wiping off the bar in order to avoid eye contact with his confidant.

Kyle long ago recognized humanity's insatiable desire for validation. However, like many realizations made by both greater and lesser men, the fact of the matter is that the realization of a seemingly universal human characteristic does not exempt the individual from falling into the trap of that characteristic. Despite Kyle's constant realization of other people's insatiable desire for validation, he finds himself in the same trap that he witnesses, and disapproves of, in so many others. Breathing heavy from the rapid-fire thoughts and his concern over what his friend might think, he is surprised to hear the response.

Neither surprised at the youthful vigor nor at the young man's assumption that he would be doubted, the old man poses what he perceives to be the only relevant question. With slouching shoulders that seem oblivious to the extent to which this idea has been weighing on Kyle's conscience, he inquires, 'Well, what have you written?'

Surprised by the candor, and taken off guard by the most obvious question he has not once considered, Kyle cautiously replies after hemming and hawing a bit. 'Nothing, other than some journal entries, letters, and an occasional poem.'

With a smile on his face, and a twinkle in his eye, the old man finds the words for the most refreshing concept Kyle will ever hear. 'That's your problem then, Kid. You won't be a writer until you've written something. Now how about another beer?'

'Thanks for that incredible insight. Where would I be without you? You're wise behind your years.' Kyle pauses, immediately regretting his tone, but is still frustrated with the cavalier attitude his compatriot has espoused. He refills the only beer glass on the bar and continues to prepare for the first chime uttered by the front door bell.

After all his preparations have been done, Kyle sits at the bar next to his friend and begins reciting the story of his childhood where he broke into the Roman house only to find himself terrified at his own reflection. LT takes the story with a hearty chuckle and turns to smile at the young bartender, who doesn't even notice.

'It took a long time to realize, but I think that story just points out how afraid I am of myself. I hope this doesn't come off in a cocky way, but I've always been good at everything I've tried and mediocre at anything I've not tried. I skated through school and jobs without much of an effort and I've never really put myself entirely into anything. I've always been rather afraid of myself.'

'That's one hell of a realization Kid.' LT takes a long sip from his beer, and continues, 'I used to be afraid of seeming imperfect. I used to kill myself at school and my jobs like I was proving something to someone. One day I got sick of it. Then I realized that all these years I hadn't been perfect.' He takes a sip of beer and pauses before continuing. 'See, true perfection seems imperfect, but it has a leg up on those things that seem perfect because true perfection is perfectly itself.' As if repeating for his own peace of mind the mantra he'd long ago forgotten, the old man mutters, 'If nothing else, true perfection is perfectly itself.'

CHAPTER TWELVE
RUNNING THE GAMUT

With a fresh beer in front of him, LT finds it nearly impossible to come clean with what is on his mind. He has been thinking about, and successfully avoiding, this moment ever since he met the young bartender, but even a dam can only hold back for so long. Eventually cracks began to show and with one strong push, LT elects to destroy the dam and let the water run free.

As if out nowhere, LT jumps to his feet and leans over the bar, looking Kyle in the eye. 'Alright Kid, this is the most important question you'll ever answer.' Kyle receives this preface with a smile as he has the impression that the old man is kidding. He would have had a much more grave expression on his face if he knew it would be the last question LT would ever ask him. 'Forget everything about a career or practicalities. I need to make it clear that you don't have to answer this question to me. I just think it's important that you ask it of yourself before making any life-changing decision.' With a sigh and a nod from Kyle, LT takes a sip of his beer and mulls over the question that has ruined both friendships and a marriage due to the average person's disgusting inability to answer it combined with LT's utter dissatisfaction with a lack of a response. With some hesitation, he inquires, 'What exactly is it that you want out of life?'

Not fully conscious of the fact that it was this question that had kept him awake so many nights, Kyle finds the words on and off his tongue before he can consider them. As if an explosion of thoughts from within finally reached a breaking point, the young man begins to impart on his friend all that had been in his mind for years. 'It sounds immature and silly but I just want to make a significant difference in the world, and before you start telling me it's impossible, I've heard it *all* about how people can't make an actual difference in the world. I've been told all about how 'there are no great men, just men who stand on the shoulders of giants' and I think it's bullshit. I think all that nonsense is a way to keep people content in their little consumer-driven, new-car-driving, mansion-house-building bubbles. It's a way to pacify the masses. I watch people in stores and walking down the street and I just fume at the sheep. I've thought about this for the last few years and there's one thing that I've come to learn.' Kyle pauses for a second to consider the fact that he's never uttered the words aloud and he's unsure how it will fall on ears that are not his own. 'Well, I say that I want to change the world and I truly believe that it's possible, but there's one thing that people don't understand. To me, changing the world isn't about making furniture stick to walls or making the masses stop buying crap they don't need. It's not about turning society on its ear. It's not about having my name in history books a hundred years from now. It's not about results. To me, changing the world is about *trying* to change the world and dying knowing you tried. It's about leaving something behind that other people can take notice of, even if all they take notice of is your effort. It's about leading by example and saying, 'I am a human being and I don't have the live like this.' It's about living your life the way you want to, not the way others see fit, not the way Wall Street says is wise, and not necessarily in a way that you feel comfortable. I think that's the most important part, being okay with being uncomfortable. It's about relishing both the uncomfortable and the comfortable. It's about experiencing the entire gamut of human emotions and encountering the entire range of human experiences. Life is about *actually experiencing* life, in whatever way you see fit, in every way you see fit. Sure, that's a lot of weight to carry around on a daily basis, but as far as I'm concerned it's the only weight that matters. The weight most people carry around is useless and carried by choice, but I'm choosing to drop the weight of debt and new clothes, the weight of a home and car for the sake of status, and the weight of what other people think of my life in order to drive this boulder to the top of the hill. I don't want to be just another sheep.'

LT, still maintaining eye contact with the young bartender, finishes his beer in one long gulp, slams down the stein and with a quiet voice begins to speak. 'Ya know Kid, I've always been of the impression that people don't think they can actually change the world.' He pauses for a moment to debate whether or not his complete thought will put fear in the heart of the young man. Knowing it has to be said, he continues, 'Most people don't think they can actually change the world, and if you think you can, they're terrified of you. They'll hate you solely for the reason that you have the gall to believe in yourself. They'll hate you because their resentment blinds them to the fact that they're jealous and it's much easier to hate someone else than it is to hate yourself.'

Kyle takes a deep breath and continues to think aloud. 'I've met so many people over the past few months working in this bar and in this town that just seem like they have so many problems with the world but no solutions. I met this guy here a few days ago that was telling me that he just gives in to all of his whims. He kinda lives by that old mantra of sex, drugs, and rock and roll. The problem is that a person like him will never change the world or even care about changing the world. If you're continually looking for your next utterly short-term temporary high, you're not looking into the future let alone considering consequences outside of that small transitory goal. It was so sad because he had no passion and was so dead inside but absolutely resigned to the fact that if he lived in a continuously orgasmic state that he would be happy. He just couldn't grasp the fact that continuous short-term happiness is not the same as true Happiness, is not the same as Peace. To me, it seems to be closer to an opposite. I guess my real problem with him wasn't the fact that he lived for the moment or that he didn't concern himself with consequences, but that he assumed that being continually high is equivalent to living in the moment. Living in the moment is about appreciating the leaves on the ground just as much as it is about appreciating the drugs in your bloodstream or the woman on your lips. It's about appreciating the lows as much as the highs.' The two men stare at each other for a solid minute without a word before the silence becomes unbearable and Kyle continues. 'Anyway, the other day I wrote a letter to my ex-girlfriend and I started thinking about how pathetically romantic I used to be. While I miss the excitement of a romantic relationship, I'm starting to think that I was just addicted to drama and excitement. I was always jumping from one bed to the next, addicted to that feeling. I guess in that sense, I was just as bad as the Man of the Moment but I hid from that realization behind flowers, poetry, and romance rather than sex and drugs.'

While Kyle doesn't frequently drink alcohol, especially this early in the day, he finds himself craving a beer so as he stands to fill the stein in front of LT, he also fills a glass for himself. 'And then the other day this guy comes in and he's being such an asshole about everything. I don't know if you remember him or not, but he just tore everything and everybody down to make himself feel better. Later on, I couldn't shake the feeling that he was just distracting himself from the fact that he's not doing anything to make this world a better place. Anyone can mock everything, but that doesn't really matter. He has no passion about anything other than negativity and I dunno, it doesn't seem like there's much that's worse for the world than that state of mind. All these people, myself included, trapped in their world of addiction to such fleeting feelings of drugs, love, sex, validity, and nobody's really doing anything to make things better. I want to change that. Maybe I can't change the world, but I can change myself.' His thoughts trail off with his voice and LT allows them to as he simply sits, willing to listen, with a cold beer in his hands.

In his own little world, Kyle is completely oblivious to whether someone else is trying to engage him in conversation. Seemingly out of nowhere he is reminded of a situation that happened when he was working at the grocery store that seems oddly appropriate to what he is attempting to express. 'My job before this was at a grocery store up the street. I didn't mind it all that much. But one day I'm stocking shelves in the cereal department and this old guy comes up to me and asks me where the Corn Flakes are. I showed him and went back to work, but he followed me while I stocked the shelves and started talking. 'When I was a kid there were two different kinds of cereal: Corn Flakes and Frosted Flakes. Now you have an entire isle for cereal. Just look, there's hundreds of em.' I looked at the old man wondering if there was more to the story, but his face grew despondent and in a really sad way he looked me in the eye and asked, 'Do you think people are any happier?' He nodded a few times at his own thought, patted me on the back and walked away with his Corn Flakes. It was incredible.' Remembering that he was communicating with another person and not just ranting to himself, Kyle brings himself back to the conversation. 'That guy was definitely not just another sheep.' The unlikely pair look up when they hear the front door bell ring as a group of men enter the bar in a perfectly formed line, in suits and ties.

Leaning over to Kyle before he takes a step in the direction of the patrons, with a smile, LT quips, 'Here comes the flock. Go tend to them, Bo Peep.'

CHAPTER THIRTEEN
AVERAGE JOE AND
THE IDEALISTIC YOUTH

It is early in the evening, the following day, when Kyle shows up forty-five minutes late to work for no real reason other than the mental distraction that has overtaken him since his conversation with LT. Not concerned with his employee's lack of punctuality, Jake takes off his apron, hands it to Kyle with a smile and a nod, and walks out of the bar without saying a word.

Kyle steps into his role as bartender as soon as the ties are tight on his smock and begins clearing tables and pushing in chairs due to the fact that there is only a handful of customers, all with apparently full drinks.

Aside from the always-booming end of the bar, only one four-top is half-filled. At the table just a few feet away from the bar are two gentlemen. One of the men appears to be in his mid forties and is wearing a tailored suit. He

111

drinks a Gin and Tonic roughly every half-hour. The other is a young man in his twenties who is obviously living the path less traveled. He sits in beat up clothes, consuming a beer every twenty minutes or so.

While the discussion is confrontational, the tone is relaxed and reserved. Kyle has heard many conversations in the bar, but never has he seen two men so engrossed in their conversation, and even more, in what the other is saying. It is as if they met at Jake's specifically to have this interaction for Kyle's eavesdropping enjoyment. From the best of his hearing, he gathers that they are discussing the businessman's job and how he dislikes it, but is still willing to work there in order to put food on his family's dinner table. Anxiously awaiting a chance to respond, the young man jumps in at the first pause he finds.

'See, my problem with people that live their lives like you is simple. To me, you represent the death of the human spirit. With your upper-middle class snobbery and your lack of an ambition that goes further than your pocketbook and your trust fund, how is society ever going to benefit from you? Sure, maybe your life is better now that you have a well-paying job. Now you can afford all those things you always wanted, but you need to ask yourself one question: is what I'm doing making the *world* a better place in any sense whatsoever?' Looking up, he sees an absolutely empty response save for attentive ears, so he continues, 'Maybe your job will allow you to feed your family, and I have no problem with that. It's entire admirable. However, what kind of example are you setting for your children? More importantly, what kind of example are you setting for mankind? Your kids are going to grow up to be just like you. They're going to be hard-working, red-blooded, active and engaged members of this corporate slave state. So you go ahead with your white picket fence and never contribute anything for the betterment of the world. The problem with you is that you've become your father, and his father before that, and his father before that. And while they may have been good men, and you may very well be a very decent man, you're not ever going to be a great man because great men see past the lifestyle that you're living and see to it that they do something to effect something outside their own perception of the world. That's the lesson this country needs to learn.'

'Hold up, hold up, hold up. Get off your soapbox for a second. Above anything else, this country is founded on my right to attain my American Dream. *My* American Dream, not yours. Call me silly or naive, call me a pawn or a slave of corporate America, but if my American Dream is a white picket fence and two-point-five kids with a lovely stay-at-home wife and a dog named Fido, who are you to call this is a lowly, selfish, or shallow dream? If nothing else, this country was founded on the proposition that I'm allowed to have my American Dream despite how you judge it. So long as I'm not hurting anyone, what's it to you that I want to live like *Leave It To Beaver*. Who are you to judge me? Because I don't live like a hobo, like a bum, my lifestyle and life choices are inferior? Because my goals aren't guided by ridiculous artistic sentiments, I'm shallow? Because my aspirations aren't directed by some overdramatic manifestation of literature's sappy sense of Love, my choices are second-rate? Well pardon me for saying so, but fuck you.'

Recognizing the young man's mouth forming a rebuttal, the older gentleman in the suit continues before any statement can reach his counterpart's lips. 'No, let me finish. You have no right to compare yourself to me in any way, shape, or form. I was raised to work hard for what I want and I've worked my ass off to get where I am now. So I drive a nice car and have a sexy wife. This makes me an inherently horrible person? See, the problem with dreamers like you is that you don't have any sort of grasp on reality. You set unattainable goals for yourself and then wax on and on about how people like me are sellouts. I've earned my place in this society. Can you honestly say that you've ever earned anything in your life? Maybe I won't save the world, but your dreams aren't going to save the world either, so at least I'm making this world a better place for the people who I care for most; my family.'

'Now wait a minute here, you're twisting around what I'm saying entirely. I'm not saying that it's shallow to care for your family or that the fact that you've worked your way through life makes you a bad person. I'm all for the idea of letting a man choose his own way of life so long as he actually and honestly weighs the pros and cons of it and makes an informed decision. My problem with your American Dream is not that you drive a nice car or have a sexy wife. It doesn't concern me that you've earned your way into a good tax bracket. While I agree that you have the right to live your life the way you wish, you give the impression that you have the obligation to attain your American Dream at the expense of virtually everything.'

'Stop right there. What do you think I've given up to get where I am? It's not as if I sold my soul for a big paycheck and a nice house.'

'But you did. You most certainly did. When's the last time you did something solely for the sake of doing it? When's the last time you created something solely for the purpose of creation? You say you haven't lost your soul, but I still maintain that you have given up your spirit to live. You're no longer living, Joe, you're surviving. You're surviving! I'm sure you'd agree wholeheartedly that life isn't about yachts and mansions. Even if you're lying to yourself, I'm sure you'll grant me this point, no?'

In a slightly dejected tone, Joe concedes, 'Of course.'

'Okay, if life isn't about yachts and mansions, then you would no doubt agree that life isn't about money.'

'Surely it's not. But I don't see where you're going with this.'

Pausing for a second to debate whether or not the time is ready to ask the big question, he begins to crack his knuckles. Noticing a lull in the conversation, Kyle brings them each another drink and because he is enjoying the conversation so much, informs them it is on the house.

Smiling as if the free beer gives him the green light he was looking for, the young man gets back on his soapbox and finishes his thought. 'This is where I'm going. I'm going to ask you something, but I don't want you to answer immediately, I want you to think about it. I want you to really think about it. Can you promise me that?' Joe nods in the affirmative. 'Alright, this question has several parts. First, if life isn't about money, yachts, and mansions as we have both come to agree, why did you put in all those overtime hours to buy that new wave-runner? Now, I told you to think about this because I don't want you just spouting off that it's a nice present for your son and that you'll use it to bond with him. You know that I'll only respond that all those extra hours you worked could have been spent with your son rather than donating your time to your employer as a means to an end which you could have readily achieved. Secondly, if life isn't about money, yachts, and mansions, what is life really about? To put it in a more specific way, if some omnipotent being were watching your life, when you died, what would he say was the point, the meaning, of your life? And don't tell me that it's about family and love because, again, look at all the overtime hours that could have been spent with them rather than your co-workers. Really Joe, what's the purpose of your life?'

Looking up to see Joe's face masking absolute, unadulterated fear, the young man understands that he can no longer do anything for the suit at the table. Perceiving that the ball is no longer in his court, and well aware that any sort of a goodbye or thanks for the conversation are not necessary, he leaves fifteen dollars in tattered and torn singles on the table, enough to cover both tabs and a generous tip. As he forces the door open he looks over his shoulder to see the man in the suit alone at the table with his head in his hands.

Joe sits at his table until the bar closes, ignoring his beeping cell phone around midnight, and turning it off around one. It isn't until Kyle begins to turn up chairs and place them on the tables in order to sweep that Joe discerns he is the only patron left in the establishment. Without thinking of the fact that the young man had paid his tab hours ago, Joe leaves a few crisp bills on the bar including a sizeable tip before exiting. As Kyle follows Joe to the door to lock up behind him, he wonders where Joe will go from that conversation.

Two days later Kyle finds out about Joe when he walks in the bar with a clean, brand new black suit, orders a martini with top-shelf liquor, and begins engaging in a one-way conversation with the regulars on the stools at the end of the bar about the features of his new BMW. They smile, sip their cheap watered down beer, and ignore the exuberant gentleman. After his drink, he takes leave of the alcoholics to get home to his wife for a home-cooked meal. Before leaving, he stops at the bar to pay his tab. Kyle gives him his change and searches for the resolve to ask the well-dressed gentleman what he can't get out of his head.

As Joe walks towards the door, he hears the bartender calling him. 'Excuse me, sir.' Joe turns to find the bartender making eye contact with him. 'A few days ago you were in here with a young man and had a long conversation. He looked strangely familiar. Could you tell me what his name was?'

Pondering for a few seconds, as if slapped back to reality, he finally responds, 'I can't for the life of me remember what that kid's name was. He asked to join me when we walked in the bar together. Real nice. A little nutty, but smart. No, sorry, I don't remember.'

'Is there anything you remember about him that might help me figure it out?' Kyle asks with an inexplicable sense of anticipation.

'Not really. All I remember is that the fool told me he had dropped out of law school. He ranted on and on about some kid burning a diploma and people's expectations of him. He was a bright kid though. Would have made one hell of a lawyer, that's for sure. You can't even imagine the things he almost had me convinced of.'

'Well, thanks anyways. Have a goodnight.'

'No problem. Take care barkeep.'

With a newfound appreciation, Kyle recalls the brief interaction on the steps of the law school when he was burning his diploma all those months ago. Perhaps one cannot affect the world with an act, but one can surely affect one person.

CHAPTER FOURTEEN
FOND FAREWELL TO A FRIEND

Snow has been falling since the early morning and has had little chance to be compacted under the feet of pedestrians. The streets are empty and many of the local stores are closed. It is the first morning since winter began with a few feet of snow, reminding everyone that summer is a long ways away, and Kyle begins the trek to Jake's bar, stepping high to get through the snow banks. While making his way to work, he watches his breath turn to frost with each exhalation. He doesn't have to open this morning, so when the bell jingles and his boss sees him standing there, Jake is confused, wondering if there was a miscommunication. With one look at the young man, he is immediately aware that he will be on the hunt for a new bartender after today.

'So where you going, Kid?' he asks as he wipes down the bar.

Slightly taken by surprise, but realizing he has with him both a stuffed backpack and a piece of luggage, Kyle merely smiles and apologizes without answering the question.

'No need for apologies. Just give me a ring if you're ever back in town. This place will always have a spot for you.'

Appreciating Jake's tact in not forcing out his plans, Kyle smiles again and sits at the bar for a few minutes thinking of all the people he's met and all the faces he will soon forget. He breathes in the stale aroma of the slightly filthy establishment, which comes predominately from the beer-soaked rubber mats behind the bar. A hint of regret arrives as he realizes that he will actually miss the wretched smell, but it quickly passes and is replaced by the determination he's worked up since the night prior.

Yesterday after his shift, Kyle walked the town for hours in the freezing cold snowfall with his mind churning faster than he could contemplate. Finally, with tired legs and frost bit hands, he went home to painstakingly write for the remainder of the evening. In fact, today he is functioning on a mere hour of sleep. However, it was the most relaxing and refreshing rest he could imagine. It was the sleep of a man who no longer wonders about his future or his past, but finds solace in the knowledge that he is committed to what he is going to do upon sunrise. It was the sleep of a man with no worries despite the fact that he is facing such uncertainty. It was no longer the sleep of an anxious youth, but the arrival of a Man.

Before departing, Kyle places a large manila envelope on the bar and asks Jake to pass it along to LT. Not realizing that Kyle had struck a friendship with the old drunk, Jake is confounded by this request but agrees to do so without a hint of hesitation. He shakes the youngster's strong hand and watches him walk out, knowing that he has lost the best worker he will find.

For a second, Jake selfishly wishes that whatever Kyle is going to do will fail in order for him to end up back at the bar, but he quickly brushes away this thought, and before the door's bell rings he yells. 'Hey Kid.' Shaken out of the concentrated daze he has maintained all morning, the young ex-bartender turns around to see his smiling ex-employer. 'Best of luck.' Kyle nods thankfully, smiles, and listens one last time to the bell on the bar door with overwhelming nostalgia. He slowly strolls to the bus station and buys a ticket.

Where the bus is going bears no importance to Kyle, and should therefore arouse no feelings of curiosity or importance in the reader. Kyle is going to end up wherever he feels comfortable and he will call that place home, for the time being.

Late that evening, LT enters his favorite bar and is surprised to find Jake serving drinks. By this point, he is well versed his young compatriot's schedule and is rather disappointed to find the gruff old man who frequently kicks him out. He sits at his usual spot and orders a beer. Much to his surprise, he finds a large yellow envelope next to his beer when he returns from the men's room. He immediately understands what has happened and sips his drink without greatly considering the envelope. He merely looks up at the bartender and asks, 'Where'd he go?'

Feeling sorry for the old drunkard, Jake fills the glass three quarters full, as he always does when giving away drinks, and hands it to LT. 'On the house. He didn't say.' Jake turns around and goes to the back room to change a keg. After tapping the large steel barrel, he sits for a second in the cooler and thinks about his young employee. Simultaneously a tear wells up in his eye and a smile edges its way across his face. 'Good for him,' he thinks, 'good for him.'

Back in a dark corner booth of Jake's bar, LT opens the envelope bearing his name. It contains a short note on top of a stack of a few pages.

LT,
The first time I met you I thought you were a stupid
old drunk. I even nicknamed you the Drunkard. I'm

124

*not saying that I was wrong, but I want you to know
that I appreciate the conversations we've had over
the past few weeks. Last night I decided I had to
leave immediately because if I didn't I would end up
tending bar for the rest of my life. I've saved up a
small sum of money and I'm getting on a bus and
going somewhere new. I'll rent out a room and I'll
write. Maybe I'm an idealistic naive child, but I
can't shake the inspiration I've so recently felt. I
won't live my life without trying something I feel so
inexplicably drawn to. Rather than being afraid of
what could happen to me, I'm jumping into life with
everything I have.*

*I need you to know that much of the courage came
from our conversations and something you said has
stuck with me for a few days now. At first I brushed
it off as the banter of a drunk old lunatic, but the
more I thought about it the more I realized the
glimmering truth in it. You said that I won't be a
writer until I've actually written something. Being a
writer isn't about living like Dostoyevsky, Throeau,
Bukowski, or Hemmingway. Being a writer is about
actually writing, and giving whatever it is you have
to offer. A friend of mine used to say something to
me as a kid that seems appropriate. He used to say,*

'There's no such thing as trying. There's doing and not doing.' I always thought that it was pretty harsh and I couldn't shake the thought that what really matters is that you try. Well even if it doesn't apply anywhere else in life, it applies here and now. There is no trying to write. There is simply writing, and not writing; doing and not doing.

I'll send you my address once I find a place. I'll send it to Jake's. Thanks for all the help, old-timer. Oh, I almost forgot. I'm sure you're wondering what the rest of the pages are. Well, I had an idea for a story and I'm running with it. I think you'll be able to appreciate it. Have a drink on me.

Farewells Aren't Forever,
Kyle

Smiling the entire time, LT uses the few dollars in the envelope to pay for his earlier beer. He hands the money to Jake who cashes him out and is surprised that on such a cold day the old drunk is leaving so early. 'Got big plans for tonight?' Jake asks.

'Naw, nothing big.' The old man mutters as he empties his pockets into the tip jar. 'Just a little bit of reading.'

126

Feeling somewhat lost, LT wanders around town for the remainder of the day. Eventually he finds a park and decides to settle there for the meantime. He brushes off the bench and takes a seat. The cold stings his face as he pulls, from the envelope, a large packet of pages. He reads for a few minutes, slowly and carefully, and turns the page to find the final paragraph. It reads:

As the last bit of ash is captured by the spring's swirling winds, a student approaches Kyle and asks what he has burned. Without seeing the face of the man who's inquiry brings him back from his meditation, Kyle replies after some thought, 'Recognition of everyone's expectations of me.' Baffled, the student stares at the gentleman on the pavement for a second before walking into the school with books under his arm. Glancing up and seeing only the back of the future nobleman or magistrate, he feels nothing but pity. Kyle looks at the black mark on the pavement and smiles before making his way back to his car, with molting feathers floating behind him in the spring breeze.

The night grows colder with every minute, but the old man finds himself surprisingly comfortable. As the evening wears on, the old man begins to violently cough for what seems like hours at a time. Tonight, with a smile on his face, LT finds comfort in the normally cold embrace of death. Like the bird he once held in his hands, he ceases to struggle against life and death, but accepts both as a gift. On the bottom of the manuscript, which his only friend has given him, unaware of exactly what he is doing, LT, the Drunkard, composes the only poem of his lifetime:

> *I'm just one measly light*
> *I can only show so much*
> *Can only effect so many*
> *I give light without effort*
> *I teach without speaking*
> *I will not allow myself*
> *To be put out*
> *Not for a day*
> > *For an hour*
> > *For a minute, or a second*
> *My radiance is constant*
> *My effect is consistent*
> *I am strong and confident*
> *Making a difference*
> *Lighting up one section of one room.*
> *I am a light*
> *One measly light*
> > *And I make all the difference in the world.*

dankennedy is an author and singer/songwriter from the suburbs of Detroit, Michigan. His literary works include a collection of short stories, titled *The Whore In Red Lipstick,* which also included stories by Joe O'Connor. More information on *dankennedy* can be found through his music website at myspace.com/dankennedymusic or by contacting him via email, DanPatKennedy@gmail.com.

3475517

Made in the USA